'Welcome to my
Sara.'

Pride stiffened her spine; pride, and the knowledge that a trap had been sprung. After swallowing to ease her arid throat, she said, 'I won't say it's a pleasure to be here.'

'I didn't expect you to.' Eyes the colour and warmth of polished steel raked her face, summoned scorching heat to her skin as his gaze drifted downward.

She'd dressed carefully for this. Although her clothes were outwardly demure, the neckline revealed the lovely lines of her throat and her every breath subtly called attention to the curves of her breasts beneath the silver mesh.

A cold haze of jealousy clouded his brain. According to the firm that was running surveillance on her, she hadn't gone out with anyone else in the past year, but her salary wasn't enough to buy clothes like this.

Unbidden memories swamped his mind—of her beneath him, soft and warm and silken, of her little gasping cries as she climaxed around him, the scent of her skin and the silken cloak of her hair, the way her voice changed from crisp confidence to an enchanting husky shyness when he made love to her, the way she laughed—

Ruthlessly Gabe re-imposed control over his unruly body.

Robyn Donald has always lived in Northland in New Zealand, initially on her father's stud dairy farm at Warkworth, then in the Bay of Islands, an area of great natural beauty, where she lives today with her husband and an ebullient and mostly Labrador dog. She resigned her teaching position when she found she enjoyed writing romances more, and now spends any time not writing in reading, gardening, travelling, and writing letters to keep up with her two adult children and her friends.

Recent titles by the same author:

THE ROYAL BABY BARGAIN
THE BLACKMAIL BARGAIN
THE BILLIONAIRE'S PASSION
BY ROYAL COMMAND
HIS PREGNANT PRINCESS

BY ROYAL DEMAND

BY

ROBYN DONALD

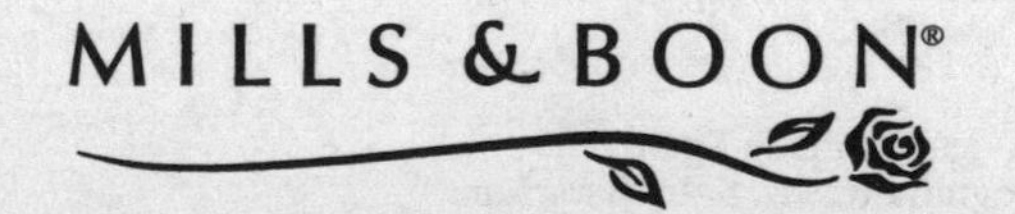

First published in Great Britain 2006
Harlequin Mills & Boon Limited,
Eton House, 18-24 Paradise Road, Richmond, Surrey TW9 1SR

Standard ISBN 0 263 84829 9
Promotional ISBN 0 263 85116 8

Set in Times Roman 10½ on 12¼ pt.
01-0706-49785

Printed and bound in Spain
by Litografia Rosés, S.A., Barcelona

CHAPTER ONE

GABE CONSIDINE looked up from his desk, his hard steel-blue eyes meeting those of his younger brother. 'So tell me I'm crazy,' he invited him curtly.

Marco's frown turned into wry amusement. 'You're crazy.'

Gabe got to his feet and strode across to the window, looking out across the walls, still intact, that surrounded the castle. For almost a thousand years his forebears had lived in the Wolf's Lair and protected the trade route crossing the mountains between the rest of Europe and the small principality of Illyria on the Mediterranean Sea. Forty years previously, civil war, treachery and death had driven his grandparents, the incumbent Grand Duke and Duchess, to fight with partisans in the mountains until their deaths in an ambush. Although Gabe and his siblings had been born in exile, Marco knew that he felt a strong sense of obligation to the people who had suffered so long, secretly hoping that their lord would come back to them.

Gabe's richly textured voice showed no emotion when he said, 'Then come up with a better idea.'

'What about good old-fashioned threats?' Marco's voice deepened into a music-hall villain's sneer. 'Tell me where the necklace is or I'll bankrupt you and throw your mother out into the snow.'

'Her mother's dead. And threats will be more effective if she's here, unable to get away.'

'A prisoner, you mean,' Marco said flatly.

Gabe shrugged. 'It wouldn't be the first time a woman's been held prisoner here.'

'Mostly they were hostages rather than prisoners.'

Gabe, Marco and their sister had grown up steeped in stories of their Illyrian heritage. One such hostage had joined the ranks of their ancestors by marrying the ruling Grand Duke.

Marco asked, 'What if Sara refuses to admit she stole the necklace?'

Gabe lifted a black brow to devastating effect.

'Then I'll do whatever's necessary to get the Queen's Blood back.'

The stark, medieval name of the necklace containing some of the most valuable rubies in the world still lifted the hairs on Marco's skin. 'Strange that any woman would happily wear something with a name like that.'

His brother gave a sardonic smile. 'Women like pretty things, even those with a barbaric history. And the Queen's Blood is more than pretty—it's magnificent, unique and irreplaceable. Flawless rubies that size are no longer being mined. And then there's the mystery of how they got from Burma to Europe, and who set them in solid gold. Some unknown Dark Age genius? Or is the necklace the sole remaining work of an unknown civilisation?'

Marco gave a snort of laughter. 'Come on, now, don't tell me you believe that old story—that it was made in Atlantis?'

His brother's mouth twisted cynically. 'Hardly. But, given all that, not many women would care that the original owner died on the mountainside a few kilometres from here, stabbed in the heart by the leader of a band of brigands. Of late, I find I have some sympathy with him.'

Marco understood the cold self-derision in his brother's tone. Falling in love with a woman, only to have her steal the priceless Considine heirloom, was definitely *not* like his cynical, hard-headed brother, noted around the world for his ruthless logic and brilliance. Oh, Gabe had had affairs, but they were always discreetly conducted, and the thought of him actually falling in love was—well, difficult to imagine!

It had been an unlikely romance—a man of ancient heritage with the world at his feet, and a woman from nowhere, struggling to make a career as an interior designer.

Yet Gabe had taken one look at Sara Milton and fallen head over heels, breaking every rule in his book with a whirlwind courtship pursued almost entirely in the full spotlight of the world's media.

Two weeks after their engagement had been announced to an incredulous public, he'd insisted that Sara wear the Queen's Blood at a ducal wedding in the south of France.

It was a night he'd never forget, Marco thought grimly, and not only because the rubies' dramatic beauty, glowing with fiery glamour in heavy, exquisitely worked gold, had set off Sara's dark hair and smoky grey-green eyes superbly. Each magnificent stone had been a perfect foil for her pale, matt skin.

That night the necklace had disappeared, stolen from a safe in the château Sara was staying at—a safe she'd chosen the combination for.

It still made Marco furious that she'd tried to blame the maid, but Gabe had seen through her ploy.

Although the theft had been kept secret, three days later

a brief, uncommunicative announcement of the termination of the engagement between Gabe Considine and Sara Milton had set the media on fire again. Some of the more delirious tabloids had called it the scandal of the century.

Marco met Gabe's hard, intelligent gaze. 'You're still absolutely certain she took it? There was no hard evidence to connect her with the theft, after all, and you'd know if she'd tried to sell it.'

In a tone that warned his brother to go no further, Gabriel said, 'She stole it.' He cut off Marco's next observation with a crystalline glance. 'If she hasn't sold it, it's because she doesn't dare to. I plan to convince her it will be worth her while to return it to me.'

Oh, Gabe could do that, Marco thought, a note in the cold voice making him even more uneasy. His brother's potent charisma was based more on his formidable personal authority than the interesting mixture of princely and aristocratic bloodlines that had bequeathed him that autocratic face and the lean, powerful body standing well over six feet.

If anyone could seduce the heirloom's whereabouts from Sara, Gabe could.

Nevertheless, Marco felt obliged to point out, 'She was going to marry you, Gabe. She could have had the Queen's Blood permanently.'

'She'd already changed her mind about that,' Gabe told him, his lips twisting in self-derision.

Only Marco and Gabe's head of security—and one photographer—knew what his brother referred to: a damning shot snapped with a telephoto lens from outside the château where Sara had been staying the night the necklace disappeared.

It showed Gabe's fiancée locked in the arms of the château's owner, Hawke Kennedy. Both were naked, and the shot had been taken through the window of Sara's bedroom.

The day after the Queen's Blood had been stolen, the picture had arrived in Gabe's e-mail with a threat to sell the negative to the highest bidder if a ransom wasn't paid.

Marco said, 'Has your security expert made any progress in finding out who the photographer was?'

'Yes.'

'I gather he won't be publishing the photograph, no matter what happens?'

Gabe's smile was as narrow and lethal as the blade of a knife. 'No.'

'So why didn't you tell him to publish and be damned? I'd have said you'd be the last man on earth to let yourself be blackmailed into paying a ransom.'

'Pride,' Gabe said shortly. 'Once it was confirmed to be genuine, I felt a complete fool for letting myself be conned into an engagement by a beautiful, clever thief. I resent being turned into an idiot by my own hormones.'

Marco said nothing, and after a moment his brother continued in the same dispassionate voice. 'Apart from that, just before the theft Alex had suggested that I come back to Illyria and be confirmed as Grand Duke of the Northern Marches.'

Marco lifted his brows. 'So?'

'Once I broke off the engagement the newspapers had a field day.'

Marco grimaced. 'Don't remind me—*the scandal of the century*! But what did Alex's proposition have to do with that—or the photograph?'

'It complicated the situation.' Gabe shrugged. 'The Illyrians—especially here, in the mountains—still believe that they need to be led by strong men. As you well know, they've got fairly rigid ideas on the respective roles of men and women. The broken engagement was bad enough. If it became known that I'd fallen for a woman who slept with another man while she was plotting to steal the Queen's Blood, the peasants would totally lose respect for me.' He gave a short, humourless laugh. 'Fair enough, but if I'm to do anything for them I need respect.'

'So even then you were seriously thinking of taking up Alex's suggestion?'

Alex, their several-times-removed cousin, had been crowned hereditary Prince of Illyria a few years previously by the determined and overwhelming will of the people. He now used his money and prestige to set his small realm, blighted by years of repression, onto the road to prosperity.

'Yes,' Gabe said. 'It will be announced in a couple of weeks.'

Marco whistled. 'So Sara missed out on being a Grand Duchess,' he observed thoughtfully.

A singularly unpleasant smile curved Gabe's mouth. 'Sad, isn't it?'

'Why did you decide to take it on?' Marco asked curiously. 'You don't need the power, and I know the title doesn't mean much to you beyond a certain sentimental attachment to our ancestors. And you certainly don't need any more money—not that it looks as though the estate's going to produce anything for years. It's just going to be a drain on your purse.'

Gabe had a big purse; like Marco, he'd carved out an empire in the piratical world of modern business with the zest and forceful flair their ancestors had devoted to keeping their turbulent lands in order. But the valley Marco had flown over that morning looked like something from a medieval print, with people huddled in tiny villages and no signs of modernisation beyond the military road the dictator had built through the pass.

Gabe shrugged and looked out over the valley, its serene beauty hiding the grinding poverty. 'Every peasant in this valley was punished over and over again by the dictator because they were loyal to our grandparents. I owe them.'

Marco nodded. Responsibility was Gabe's big thing. 'You could help them without reverting to feudalism and becoming a ruling Grand Duke.'

His brother said ironically, 'You know Alex's powers of persuasion—after all, he talked you into taking on his software business so he could devote himself to Illyria.'

'Yeah, he did.' Marco grinned. 'And I jumped at it. I'm having a ball. What's your excuse?'

'I've been coming here for the past year, trying to find out how I can best help these people, and they've made it plain that they want a Grand Duke, just as they wanted Alex back. It seems a psychological boost for the generation who remember the good old days, but even the younger people are eager.'

While Marco was digesting this, Gabe added caustically, 'Which is why I felt that a photograph of my nude fiancée with her latest lover would taint both the title and Alex's hard work.'

'I see your point.' Marco looked ironically at his older brother. 'You should have charged the tabloids for providing material. First they went berserk when you and Sara announced your engagement, then a fortnight later you dumped her. Talk about starting a feeding frenzy!'

Marco still found it hard to believe that Sara Milton had stolen the necklace. Or taken Hawke Kennedy for a lover. OK, Sara was beautiful in a way that got to any man with decent eyesight and the smallest drop of testosterone in his body, but he'd also liked her very much.

Still, a likeable personality would be a very useful asset for a con woman.

Without any hope of persuading his brother, he felt obliged to point out, 'If you go ahead with this crazy scheme, you'll be leaving yourself open to more blackmail. Kidnapping is an offence in Illyria, Gabe. Even Alex might not be able to save you if Sara decides to press charges.'

He watched his brother's boldly chiselled features harden. That same inflexible expression blazed from the portraits of their ancestors. Ruthless men—and women—known for their formidable, uncompromising loyalty to their prince and their superb skills in the art of war, they'd held the border with a mixture of intimidating authority and brutal intelligence.

Oh, Gabe would make a fitting Grand Duke. And he'd certainly help Alex with his plans to restore Illyria's prosperity and confidence.

Still, Marco felt distinctly wary. Gabe was the last person he'd accuse of an obsession, but his brother seemed immune to any doubts.

When Gabe spoke, his voice was cold and deep, not betraying any emotion. 'She's coming here of her own free will.'

'She doesn't know this is your castle, or that you plan to keep her here until she gives you what you want.'

Gabe smiled unpleasantly. 'Until she gives me what I *own*,' he corrected. He surveyed his brother's face. 'Relax. I don't plan to torture her or confine her to the dungeons. The minute she tells me where the necklace is she can go. And she won't go to the police—or to the media.' The icy contempt in his tone lifted the hairs on the back of Marco's neck. 'I imagine her last joust with them battered her enough to make her avoid them like the plague.' He dismissed the topic as though it meant nothing and smiled at his brother, his affection plain. 'Are you ready to go?'

'Yes. Anything you want me to relay to Alex?'

Gabe's face softened. 'Just give the baby a hug for me.'

Marco grinned. 'I'll do that. Fancy picking you to be his godfather! Still, you're good with kids.' He sobered swiftly. 'I don't like this, Gabe, but I know better than to try and talk you out of it. Just—take care, will you?'

Gabe shrugged. 'I won't need to. She's on my territory this time, and I hold all the cards. Last time I was halfway across America when I heard what had happened; she was free to do what she wanted.'

He went down to the helicopter with Marco and watched it disappear down the valley towards the coast. Strolling back into the castle, he looked around, keen eyes noting the various things that needed to be done.

His brother was too easily swayed by a lovely face that managed to be gracious and composed even when Sara Milton was lying in her teeth.

But then, why should he blame Marco for that weakness? She'd fooled him, too, and, God knew, during his meteoric rise in the world's rich list he'd rapidly learned to spot the signs of a woman intent on snaring a billionaire husband.

His arrogantly outlined mouth drew into a thin line. Yet he'd been a total idiot over Sara. In spite of his experience, he'd let himself be dazzled by her lovely face, serene eyes and passionate mouth. So much so, he'd lowered his guard enough to decide to marry her, and matched the heirloom Queen's Blood with a ruby on her finger.

More fool him!

A light flashed in the gathering dusk over the mountain, and the distant thump-thump-thump of rotors gathered strength as another helicopter swooped towards the castle. Warily, he monitored his emotions.

He felt nothing, he was pleased to realise, beyond a compelling determination to shake the whereabouts of the necklace from her. Once that was done, he'd have the greatest pleasure in throwing her out of the castle and Illyria.

And then he'd never think of her again.

CHAPTER TWO

FOR a heart-stopping second, Sara's breath caught in a shocked gasp. The light from the helicopter illuminated a fiery scarlet flow over the ancient stone walls of the castle; they looked as though they were awash with blood.

Another, closer survey revealed the outline of leaves and long ropy stems. The violent colour was merely autumn shades in an ancient vine.

'Get a grip,' she muttered, trying to quell a sudden, primitively superstitious sensation. Into her mind popped memories of vampire stories she'd read as a teenager, vivid enough to make her lift uneasy eyes to the mountains surrounding the valley.

This was ridiculous. Since Prince Alex had been restored to the throne of Illyria some years previously it had become a civilised state, open to the world. Besides, weren't vampires supposed to live in Rumania? Her mouth tilted in an ironic smile. She'd grown up on a small Pacific island, and her knowledge of their natural habitats was limited to the books she'd borrowed from her mother's employer.

Anyway, she wasn't going to be here long; all she had to do was check out three bedrooms and bathrooms and come up with a brilliant plan to redecorate them, one that kept the medieval ambience intact while incorporating modern plumbing.

If only it were that easy, she thought, fear gnawing beneath her ribs. She was desperate to get this commission. Winning the approval of the elegant American heiress who owned the castle might set her career back on track after the disaster of the past year.

Don't go there, she commanded herself instantly, but pain came rolling in like a grey cloud, smothering everything in the aching misery she knew so well. Sightlessly she stared down at a green lawn sheltered within the castle walls.

If the past months had taught her anything, it was that, no matter what happened, life had to go on.

The chopper touched down with a slight bump. She shivered and blinked, dragging herself out of her sombre recollections. Frowning, she peered into the dusk. She'd known the owner wasn't going to be there, but she hadn't expected the castle to be deserted. No lights shone from windows flanked by shutters painted with some heraldic outline.

'A wolf?' she muttered.

Yes, it looked like a wolf—ears, teeth and a very red tongue stood out prominently. Very rampant, she thought mordantly; definitely a wolf to be reckoned with! Sensation crawled between her shoulder-blades, setting every sense strumming.

She turned her head to inspect more blank, dark windows climbing a turreted tower. Of course she felt as though she was being watched; that was what the castle had been built to do! It loomed over the valley to guard the trade route through the mountains.

Stop letting it get to you—right now! she ordered herself sturdily, but followed the words with a muffled laugh that sounded too much like a sob. It didn't matter. The pilot was busy doing whatever helicopter pilots did just after they landed, and he didn't speak English anyway.

All she needed to finish off this interminable day was the appearance of a servant called Igor!

The door slid back, the noise of the blades assailing her ears, then easing. 'Madam?'

Ah, a human being—a short, stout man who had *butler* written all over him. And, far from being an Igor, he was an Englishman, if she'd heard his accent correctly above the roar of the rotors.

Relieved, she smiled and unclipped her seat belt and swung long legs out onto the grass, automatically ducking as he urged her away from the helicopter.

A safe distance from the rotors, he indicated an arched door in the massive stone wall. 'This way, madam.' When she hesitated he added, 'Your luggage will follow.'

He held out his hand for her heavy tote bag. Reluctantly, Sara handed it over.

The door led into a courtyard. Sara could see flowers glimmering in pots, and her tension eased as she drew in a deep breath. Fresh and wholesome, free of the mechanical taint of whatever fuel powered the chopper, the air was still suffused with warmth from the brilliant autumn day. Subduing her foolish fear, Sara straightened her shoulders and followed the butler, determined to give this commission her very best.

The cobblestones came as a surprise, their rounded, uneven surface tossing her off balance.

She recovered quickly, but the man beside her murmured solicitously, 'Not very far now, madam,' and indicated another large, solid door, clearly built to repel any invaders foolish enough to attack.

Or keep prisoners well and truly incarcerated, she

thought with an inward qualm, irritated with herself for letting her imagination run wild. The American who owned this castle had been totally *un*-sinister, a perfectly groomed, modern woman who just wanted three bedrooms turned into welcoming, elegant havens for her guests.

The heavy wooden door, armoured with an impressive medieval lock, opened onto a large stone-flagged hall.

The manservant gave her a polite smile. 'Please come in. I hope you had a pleasant journey.'

'Very, thank you,' Sara said automatically, following him into the castle.

And of course it wasn't chilly and dank inside—cool, but she'd expected that; very old furniture and artefacts suffered from central heating.

The place was immaculate. No spider webs hung from rafters, nothing gibbered in a corner…

The butler led her across the hall towards yet another forbidding door. Grim, superbly crafted suits of armour lined the walls, their hard, masculine ambience barely tempered by flowers in great urns and bowls. At the other end of the hall a banner was draped from on high. Although muted by age and wear, Sara's wondering eyes discerned the outline of a wolf.

Her skin tightened. What the hell was she doing here? Her expertise lay in houses, not this kind of architecture, with its overt statement of power and ruthlessness. She'd decorated apartments in London and the South of France, but never anything as old as a castle.

Well, it would be a challenge, and it would look damned good on her CV.

The butler held open another door and led her along a stone passage that had probably served as part of the defensive structure.

To break the oppressive silence, she said brightly, 'Does the castle have a name?'

'Why, yes, Miss Milton. The Castle of the Wolf—or, as the locals call it, the Wolf's Lair.'

Too much! 'Then the banner in the great hall must be the crest of the original owners?'

'Indeed it is,' he said, opening a small door that led into a lift.

She smiled ironically as she followed him into it. Of course the castle had a lift, which its sophisticated American owner would call an elevator. Sara hoped it wasn't the only concession to the twenty-first century!

Several floors up, the manservant showed her into a room where painted panelling overpowered a four-poster bed, its head- and footboard carved in a delicate tracery of flowers and vines. With restoration it would be charming.

Not so the rest of the room, all gilt and heavy crimson and stark white, the furniture second-rate reproductions. No wonder Mrs Abbot Armitage wanted the rooms redecorated! Whoever had perpetrated this shoddy travesty should be prevented from going anywhere near a room again, Sara thought vigorously.

Still, at least there was no sign of any wolf here. Perhaps Mrs Abbot Armitage didn't care for wolves in the bedroom.

Sara could only agree.

The manservant indicated a door in the panelling. 'Your bathroom is through there,' he told her. 'If you would like to rest for an hour or so I will return to escort you down to the drawing room for a drink before dinner.'

'Oh.' When he looked at her with an expression of mild enquiry she elaborated. 'I didn't think there was anyone here.' She stopped, because that sounded stupid. 'In residence,' she amended.

'Oh, yes,' was all he said, putting her bag down on a chair before he left.

Frowning, Sara stared at the door as it closed behind him, and decided there must have been more warmth behind the American heiress's patrician face than she'd suspected. At least she wasn't to be given a meal to eat in her room, like a Victorian governess!

But, kindness or not, Sara reminded herself that her future depended on delivering a plan for the rooms that would outdo those submitted by other decorators.

A cool shiver of foreboding tightened her skin. She looked around and noticed a casement open to the evening air.

'Stop *dramatising* everything!' she ordered herself sternly, and leaned out.

It was still light; even now, ten years after she'd left Fala'isi, she found the slow twilights of Europe enchanting. The tropical nights of the Pacific had crashed down like a pall, snuffing out the hot, brilliant colours of the island within minutes.

The air was pure, scented with a ripeness that hinted at harvest and full barns. Because the room was above the ramparts, she could look out across the valley. Small dim clusters of lights marked villages, and high on the bulk of the surrounding mountains the few pinpricks must be from isolated farmsteads.

Craning, she saw several windows glowing in one of the castle towers; as she watched, someone walked across them, pulling the curtains closed.

Some primal instinct made her cringe back. Eyes wide and strained, she watched the unknown man—probably the uncommunicative manservant—extinguish the squares of golden light.

Above her glittered stars, the constellations alien.

Growing up, she'd learned every star—and had known almost every palm tree and person on the island, she thought wistfully.

Homesickness and something more painful washed over her. However much she loved Fala'isi, there was nothing there for her now, and this was her last chance to retrieve the career that Gabe had ruthlessly derailed.

Her mouth twisted into a grimace. Not that she could trace the swift extinction of her career directly to him—he was far too subtle. But although the *nouveau riche* might have flocked to patronise a woman who'd been engaged to such a powerful man, any hint that she was a thief would have sent them fleeing.

And hint there must have been. The theft of the necklace, the famous Queen's Blood, had never reached the media, but her employer had sacked her the moment Gabe had broken their engagement.

The necklace had blighted everything she'd worked for, everything she'd loved. The most precious heirloom of Gabe's family for a thousand years. For her, she thought starkly, it was cursed.

The only time she'd worn it, at the very grand wedding of a cousin of Gabe's, a superstitious shudder had iced her spine.

Gabe had put it on her himself, and even the touch of his hands on her shoulders hadn't been able to warm her. She'd asked too quickly, 'Who made it?'

'No one knows. Some experts say it originated from a Scythian hoard,' Gabe had said, eyes narrowed and intent as he'd settled the heavy chain on her shoulders. 'They were a nomadic people from the steppes, noted for their cruelty and their magnificent work in gold. The rubies are definitely from Burma.'

She'd watched herself in the mirror, half entranced by

the necklace's beauty, half repelled by its bloody history. It had a presence, an aura made up of much more than the fact that it was beyond price, so rare it couldn't be insured.

And in spite of her heartfelt, desperate protests, Gabe had been so certain she'd stolen it he'd broken off their engagement in the cruellest way. She'd learned of it from his press release.

Even now she felt sick at the memory of the resulting media uproar, the flashbulbs, the sickening innuendoes, the lies and gossip and jokes. For three months she'd frantically searched for a new job and watched her savings dwindle.

Yet nothing had been as nightmarish as realising that the man who'd wooed her with a savage tenderness that had swept her off her feet had ruthlessly used his power and influence to ruin her life.

She'd loved Gabe so much, and, fool that she was, she'd let herself be convinced that this magnificent man loved her, too. But at the first test of his love it had been revealed to be an illusion. Her only buttress against collapse had been her pride.

And her skill as an interior designer, she reminded herself. She was *good*, damn it!

Fala'isi was as distant to her as the stars, part of a life long gone. Fortunately, after several months of desperate endeavour, one decorator had agreed to give her a chance. She owed it to him to do this properly, even though he'd made it more than clear that if there was ever the smallest slip-up she'd go. So far he'd watched her closely, but the fact that he'd let her off the leash now must mean that he was learning to trust her.

A knock on the door jerked her out of her unhappy thoughts. 'Come in,' she called.

The manservant brought in her suitcase and placed it on a stand.

'Thank you,' she said, smiling at him.

He gave a stiff nod. 'If you need anything, madam, there is a bell-pull,' he said, and left, closing the door silently behind him.

Rebuffed, Sara caught sight of herself in a mirror and shuddered. She needed a shower and she needed it *now*. Mourning the forlorn mess her life had become wasn't getting her anywhere; better to summon her energies and make this a success. And the first thing to go, she thought, should be the bell-pull, long and gold and tasselled in the most vulgar way.

The bathroom was just as depressing as the bedroom, an abomination in mock-Victorian style with gilded taps and a marble tub. And the plumbing—well, it needed first aid.

No, surgery—a major transplant, in fact. Grimly Sara washed in water that was barely lukewarm.

Back in the room she looked around, her frown deepening as she realised that her suitcase had disappeared. Heart thumping, she went across to a large armoire against one wall and, yes, there were her clothes, either stacked on the shelves or hanging. Someone—not the man who'd shown her in, she hoped—had been busy while she'd showered.

Prominently displayed on a hook inside the door were her sleek, ankle-length black skirt, a jetty silk camisole and her discreet, long-sleeved textured top, its transparent black webbed by silver mesh.

Obviously castle owners dressed for dinner. She hadn't brought high heels, but the skirt was long enough to hide the tops of her black ankle boots.

'Thank you, whoever you are,' she said devoutly to the unknown person who'd taken pity on her and hinted at suitable gear.

Once dressed, a quick glance in the mirror revealed that

she looked suitably anonymous. She made up with restraint, settling on a faint darkening of her eyes and berry-coloured lipgloss rather than the full armour. She couldn't afford, she thought cynically, to look like a woman on the make!

Carefully she pulled back her hair, pinning it into a neat, classic chignon at the back.

A tactful knock at the door set her heart slamming in her chest. Calm down, she told herself sternly. No Igor, no vampires; this is a job—and your future depends on it, so go out there and do your best.

The manservant stood back as she came through. 'This way, madam,' he said, and took her down in the lift, although not all the way to the bottom floor, then escorted her along another stone corridor.

'To the parlour,' he told her in his colourless voice. 'It is less formal than the drawing room.'

Oh, good, so this wasn't going to be a *formal* occasion.

Trying to regulate her heartbeats, she gazed discreetly around for clues to the taste of the owners. In spite of her American client, the original ancestors were still in residence; Sara met the painted eyes of one haughtily beautiful woman and wondered who she was, and why she seemed strangely familiar.

Her companion stopped outside a door and flung it open, announcing, 'Miss Milton.'

And Sara walked into the nightmare that had haunted her dreams for the past year.

After the tasteless kitsch of her bedroom, the elegant, panelled study came as a shock—but not as much a shock as the man who stood beside the marble Renaissance chimneypiece.

Gabe Considine, the man she'd loved and had been going to marry. Tall, lean, yet powerfully built, clad in the formal black and white of evening clothes, his boldly chiselled features and slashing cheekbones exuding an uncompromising impression of power and authority.

And although not a muscle in his lean, handsome face moved when he saw her, Sara sensed a dark, formidable satisfaction in him that chilled her through to her bones.

For a terrified second every muscle in her body locked into stasis, holding her frozen to the floor.

'Thank you, Webster,' Gabe said, his voice cool and autocratic. He waited until the door closed behind the man, then smiled, and drawled, 'Welcome to my ancestors' castle, Sara.'

Pride stiffened her spine; pride, and the sick knowledge that a trap had been sprung.

After swallowing, to ease her arid throat, she said thinly, 'I won't say it's a pleasure to be here.'

'I didn't expect you to.' Eyes the colour and warmth of polished steel raked her face, summoned scorching heat to her skin as his gaze drifted downward.

Cynically, Gabe decided that she'd dressed carefully for this. Although her clothes were outwardly demure, the neckline revealed the lovely lines of her throat and her every breath subtly called attention to the curves of the breasts beneath the silver mesh.

As for the straight black skirt, so simple and straight—until she took a step, and the skirt opened just above the knee to showcase a long, elegant leg.

A cold haze of jealousy clouded his brain. According to the firm that was running surveillance on her, she hadn't gone out with anyone else in the past year, but her salary wasn't enough to buy clothes like this. Second-hand? Probably; whatever, it didn't matter.

The classic hairstyle revealed her perfect features, cool

and composed except for the luscious mouth, and even that she'd toned down with a mere film of rosy colour. She wore no jewellery at all, yet the overall effect was of a woman confident of her body and her sexuality.

Unbidden memories swamped his mind—of her beneath him, soft and warm and silken, of her little gasping cries as she climaxed around him, the scent of her skin and the silken cloak of her hair, the way her voice changed from crisp confidence to an enchanting husky shyness when he made love to her, the way she laughed—

Ruthlessly Gabe reimposed control over his unruly body.

'You look well,' he said smoothly. 'Cool, sophisticated, yet businesslike. But then, image is your talent.'

He watched the colour fade from that exquisite magnolia skin. No sign of blusher, he noted.

'I hope my talent is a little more substantial than that,' she said, crisply turning the unspoken insult from herself to her work. 'I like to feel that interior decorating does more than create a pretty background. This, for example—' looking around his study '—bears no resemblance to the bedroom you've given me. I'm sure I don't need to ask you which room you feel most comfortable in.'

A quick rally; but then, people who made a living from conning others had to have instant recovery when they were caught out.

'I chose to meet you here in the study because this is how I want the rest of the castle to be,' he said smoothly. 'Appropriate is probably the best word to use. Would you like a drink?'

To his surprise she accepted, although her eyes widened when he poured champagne. She'd noticed that it was an extremely good vintage, and she was wondering what he was celebrating. Good; he wanted her unsettled.

And he'd succeeded. When she took the glass her fingers tightened for a betraying few seconds around the fragile stem.

Gabe waited, then said, on a note of caustic appreciation, 'Here's to reunions.'

Her lashes drooped over the tilted grey-green eyes, and his pulses leapt. She was, he thought with savage self-contempt, the only woman who could override his common sense with one sideways glance.

She took a swift sip of the wine, then set the glass down and turned her head to gaze into the leaping flames in the fireplace. Her hair gleamed rich mahogany against the matt satin of her skin.

'Why did you bring me here?' she asked, her voice level and toneless.

He didn't answer straight away, and after a moment she glanced back at him.

She'd lost weight, he thought with an irrational spurt of concern. 'I thought it was time we discussed things without the unnecessary complication of emotions.'

Had he got over her so soon? A swift glance at his implacable face convinced her. Of course he no longer loved her…if he ever had.

Probably their relationship had been a temporary aberration on his part. He couldn't have felt anything true or lasting.

After all, what could the scion of a princely house, a man who moved confidently in the upper regions of power and influence, have in common with a woman like her? No money, no family—no idea of her father's name, even—and no status.

She hid her pain with another sip of the champagne. But he could have been kinder—well, no. Her lips sketched a cynical little smile. He thought she'd conned him out of his most precious possession, and the huge media fall-out from their break-up would have rubbed his pride raw.

'I don't know why you set this up,' she said evenly. 'I have nothing to say to you, beyond that I don't know where the necklace is. If I'd known you were here I would never have come.'

He lifted a mocking brow. 'I find that hard to believe. You once told me that you researched your clients well before you started a job. And you knew I had links to Illyria.'

'I knew you were a cousin of the Prince, but I had no idea that you owned a thumping great castle here!' she countered. 'Anyway, you're meant to be in—'

His cold smile stopped the betraying words.

'Don't lie, Sara.' Like her Polynesian friends in Fala'isi, he pronounced her name with a long vowel—Sahra…

She'd always loved the way he said it, the two syllables falling lazily, sensuously, from his tongue like an endearment, his tone a seduction in itself.

Not now, though. He'd turned it into a hard, subtly insolent epithet.

Bitterness and anger shortened her words into sharp little arrows. 'Of course I made sure that you wouldn't be in Illyria. Why aren't you in South America at the United Nations conference?'

'Because I arranged for you to come here.'

CHAPTER THREE

GABE came towards her, silent and formidably graceful as the wolf his ancestors had been called. Only a tough involuntary pride stopped Sara from taking a backward step, and she lifted her chin to meet his eyes with as much defiant composure as she could produce. She would *not* be intimidated.

She'd done nothing wrong.

'I won't be here for long,' she retorted smartly.

'You'll stay until I send you away, Sara.'

'You can't do that!' She dragged in a sharp breath, but it failed to deliver enough oxygen to energise her stunned brain.

'I can do anything I want with you.' He waited, drawing out the silence before finishing softly. 'No one knows you're here.'

'My boss…'

His smile chilled her blood. 'He won't help.' He waited with speculative dispassion while she struggled with the implications of that confident statement.

Sara's hand clenched on the stem of her glass and a huge emptiness hollowed out her insides. Stonily she asked, 'Are you implying that you arranged my job for me?'

'Of course. I wanted you where I could keep an eye on

you.' He spoke casually, as though it was the most natural thing in the world for him to have done.

And, of course, it was.

Sara's mouth dropped open. Stunned, she gazed at him in stupefied disbelief.

The unexpected offer of a job from a respected interior designer had literally given her something to live for. To learn that Gabe had organised it, and that her work meant nothing, hurt her so deeply she couldn't speak.

She should have known, Sara thought as humiliation ate into her, leaving her cold and shaky. Gabe didn't take betrayal lightly; he was famous for his long memory and his insistence on fair play. He'd want revenge. And he had the power and the money to seek it cold, to organise it with ruthless efficiency, so that she had no way of protecting herself.

Struggling to keep a clear mind, she fought back a sense of debilitating helplessness. He'd played with her life as though she were a puppet. It hurt, and it frightened her.

Nevertheless, she wasn't going to surrender. He'd enjoy that; it would satisfy his desire to humiliate her. 'I suppose I'm no longer working for him?'

'That depends entirely on you,' he said, watching her with coldly speculative eyes. 'I want the Queen's Blood, Sara. Tell me where it is and your life will be your own again.'

Her own? She could almost have laughed if his dispassionate tone hadn't bruised so painfully. Gabe might have been able to cut her out of his life with merciless precision, but her heart was not so easily placated; it still trembled when she looked at him, longing for a commitment that had only ever existed in her wishful thinking.

If he'd loved her, he'd have at least given her a hearing when she'd tried to see him. But, no—he'd accepted the word of his grandmother's maid rather than listen to the woman he'd been planning to marry!

Knowing it was hopeless, she said in a brittle voice, 'If I knew where the rubies are, believe me, I'd have told you.'

'Listen to me,' he said forcefully, his eyes hooded and dangerous. 'It occurred to me that you might be afraid. That's why I brought you here—where you'll be completely safe.'

'Not from you!' she retorted.

His wide shoulders moved in a slight negligent shrug. 'Of course you're safe from me—I'm not a barbarian.'

'You threatened me about half a minute ago!' He wasn't going to get away with deliberately trying to intimidate her. She matched his hostile stare with one of her own, eyes glinting green as grass beneath her slim winged brows.

Another shrug underlined his Mediterranean heritage, from those warlike warriors whose blood had mingled with that of princesses from all over Europe to give him arrogantly handsome features and stunning colouring—hair like ebony, eyes as cold and blue as the sheen on a scimitar, and skin of warm bronze.

'I knew you wouldn't be intimidated,' he said coolly. 'But planning and executing a heist as successful as the Queen's Blood is one thing—selling the thing is another. That involves criminals, and where this amount of money is involved the criminals are not loveable rogues. Stop hedging, Sara—it's not getting you anywhere. Tell me where the Queen's Blood is and I'll let you go without fear of prosecution.'

The last tiny flicker of hope died. How could he be so intelligent in every other respect, yet so bone-headedly convinced that she'd stolen the necklace? Sara snatched another look at his face and saw beneath his amused contempt an unsparing determination.

Mindless panic roiled starkly beneath her ribs. She hid it by snapping, 'You meant it when you said you could do whatever you liked with me.'

His black brows drew together in a forbidding frown that revved her heart-rate up into the stratosphere. 'Oh, yes, I meant it. I could.' His voice turned sarcastic. 'But do try to restrain your vivid imagination. I don't intend to hurt you.'

'Why should I believe you?' she demanded, realising too late that attacking his credibility was hardly the best way to get him to reconsider this crazy scheme and let her go.

Anyway, it wouldn't work. Oh, Gabe definitely had a temper, but it was all the more intimidating for being so tightly controlled. More steadily she finished, 'You didn't believe me.'

'Did I ever hurt you?'

'I—no,' she admitted reluctantly. Not physically, anyway. Indeed, he'd always been exquisitely tender with her.

Her heart-rate picked up as she remembered just how tender—and how she'd gloried in his strength and his potent male sexuality.

'So stop pretending to be scared of me,' he said crisply. 'And don't try to evade the subject. If you're worried about your safety, be assured that no one can reach you here—no army has ever taken the castle by force.'

Sara remained stubbornly mute. Anything she had to say would only make things worse.

He waited, and when she didn't fill the silence, went on relentlessly. 'Give me the details of the theft and who else was involved. I promise you'll be safe.'

As he'd once promised to love her?

'I don't know what happened to the wretched necklace,' she told him, each word emerging with mechanical precision. 'I gave it to the maid—to Marya—to put in the safe, and to the best of my knowledge she did just that.'

His response was unexpected. Instead of the chilling disbelief she'd had to endure when she'd tried to convince him of this a year before, he nodded. 'And she swears that she did that, too. But about an hour afterwards she realised that she hadn't put your engagement ring there, so she slipped down from her bedroom to do that. When she got there, the safe was empty. It had been opened by someone who knew the combination, which, as you set the combination when you arrived to stay with Hawke, means that you took it.'

A raw edge in his voice alerted her. She glanced up sharply, shock freezing her brain when she saw the dangerous glitter in his eyes. Stubbornly she retorted, 'Or Marya.'

Holding her gaze, he said on a lethal note, 'Marya is completely trustworthy.'

'You're so sure of that?' she asked impetuously, knowing even as the words tumbled from her lips that she was on a hiding to nothing.

She hadn't stolen the necklace, so the thief had to be Marya. Why, she didn't understand, but there was no one else.

'I'm sure,' he said, his handsome, autocratic face hardening. 'And, as the Queen's Blood hasn't yet appeared on the market—'

'How do you know?'

Wide shoulders lifting in the slightest of shrugs, he kept his steel-blue gaze fixed on her face. She felt as though she had diamond lasers boring through the outer layer of skin and bone, right into her brain.

But if he could do that, he'd see her innocence.

He said, 'The jewellery world is small, and it's been under surveillance ever since the Queen's Blood was taken.

Apart from the value of the gold and the stones, the necklace is priceless as an artefact; an ancient, solid gold chain studded with perfectly matched cabochon rubies could only be sold to a collector. He'd have to be very rich and very unscrupulous, and have more money than sense.'

She frowned. 'Why more money than sense?'

'Because it could never be worn, never be shown—not for generations, if ever. It's so well known that it would immediately be claimed by me, or my heirs. And if my line fails, Illyria would be entitled to the thing because it was originally found here.' He stopped for a few measured seconds before adding deliberately, 'But it hasn't been bought by any collector, Sara.'

Eyes as cold and hard as ice searched her face. He thought she already knew all this; he was humouring what he considered to be her sly treachery.

Pain cramped her into rigidity. A year hadn't been long enough to chisel him from her heart. She'd loved him so much....

Without emotion, he continued, 'It could have been broken up and sold discreetly, stone by stone, on the black market. When the tyrant took over Illyria, my grandfather gave the necklace to someone to hide. After the usurper was assassinated, the only person who knew the hiding place brought it to me. I had each gem in the necklace measured and profiled, and its signature is stored. Burmese rubies the size of those in the Queen's Blood and of the very best quality and colour—pure red with the faintest undertone of blue—haven't been found for centuries. If even one such ruby turned up on the market I'd know within a few hours. It hasn't happened.'

'Because Marya doesn't want to sell it.'

Without moving a muscle, he said, 'Can you give me

one good reason why Marya, who was my grandmother's maid, would want to steal the Queen's Blood?'

During the last year Sara had cudgelled her brain, trying to think of just such a reason, and the only one she could come up with was that the Illyrian woman had believed an upstart nobody to be completely unsuitable for her lord's wife.

She was probably right.

The flames in the fireplace sprang high, then collapsed, and a faint, familiar scent reminded Sara of apples. Prunings from the orchards she'd seen beneath the helicopter, she thought, clinging to that simple sweetness in a room filled with fear and tension.

Oppressed by the weight of centuries of history, of death and war and disillusionment within the walls of the castle, she said flatly, 'I'm sorry it was stolen, but I had nothing to do with it.'

Gabe drank some wine, then put his glass down with a sharp movement that set the golden liquid surging in the flute. 'I don't believe Marya took it because she was the one who hid the necklace when my grandparents abandoned the castle.'

Astonished, she stared at him. She knew the story. The general of the revolutionary army—a man whose violence had been legendary—had threatened to kill every person in the valley if the castle was defended. Gabe's grandparents had slipped away in the night and joined the partisans, fighting in the mountains until they eventually died in an ambush.

In a thin voice she said, 'Is that why you wanted her to be my maid?'

'Partly. She asked if she could be when she heard that we were engaged. I suggested it to you because she was my grandmother's maid, and I suppose it satisfied something in me to have her take care of you and your clothes.'

Sara bit her lip.

'Yes,' he said sardonically, answering her unspoken response. 'You chose the wrong person to frame, Sara. Marya would never have stolen the necklace because she spent forty years protecting it at huge personal cost to herself and her family. She endured everything because she was loyal and because she understands the necklace's enormous symbolic value.'

'Is that why you're so determined to find it?' At least she could now understand why Gabe was so sure of Marya's innocence. Not that it helped. 'Does it confer some sort of divine right to rule on whoever holds it?'

'No,' Gabe said deliberately, surveying her with hooded, scornful eyes. 'I'm trying to explain why I know Marya didn't steal it. Whereas you lied to me and betrayed me. Give me one reason why I should believe you.'

Humiliation leached the colour from her skin. She stumbled over her next words, then caught her breath and forced herself to repeat stubbornly, 'I didn't lie or betray you.'

'All I want is the Queen's Blood,' Gabe responded indifferently, making it more than obvious he didn't believe her.

So what else was new?

He went on, 'It's an heirloom of my house, and I want it back again. Then you'll be free to go.'

The beautiful, fabulous object, rich with history and tragedy and glamour, had shattered her heart. Gabe valued it more than he'd valued her, and his so-called love hadn't withstood the suspicion that had swirled around her after the necklace had disappeared.

Sara dragged in a slow, jagged breath. 'I wish you had it,' she said, pain thinning her voice, 'but I don't know what happened to it and I can't tell you where it is. I'm sorry.'

'*Won't* tell me.' His voice was controlled and impersonal, as though he was discussing a business deal. 'I'm prepared to pay you the value of the Queen's Blood for information about its whereabouts.' He named an amount that horrified her.

Sara closed her eyes. Just how far would he take this? 'I don't know where it is,' she repeated dully.

'The offer stands. It's considerably more than you'll get from breaking up the necklace and selling the stones on the black market. And much more than you'll get from a collector who knows you don't dare offer it legally.' He picked up his glass and drank some of the champagne, his long fingers tanned and strong against the delicate transparency of the crystal stem.

They'd always been exquisitely gentle on her body. Sara turned away as memories exploded in intimate, painfully acute clarity. She tried to wall them off, but her skin tightened at the recollection of the heat of his sleek, bronzed hide against hers, the power and the rapture of impassioned hours locked in his arms, and the transcendent ecstasy of his possession.

A subtle, hidden softening deep inside her shocked her into awareness of her danger. Bitterly she forced the seductive images to the back of her mind. Oh, he'd been a magnificent lover, but he'd instantly believed that she'd stolen the necklace.

Now she understood why, but his reasons simply underlined the fragility of their relationship. For all its fire and flash and transient ecstasy, love had opened her to an anguish that would scar her for life.

'I can't help you. I'll leave now,' she said quietly, clutching at a composure so brittle she was afraid it would splinter at his next insulting word.

'You're not going anywhere.' His reasonable tone warred with the determination she saw in his handsome face.

Tension knotted inside her. Her tongue felt thick in her mouth when she said, 'You can't keep me here, and you know it.'

'You'll stay here until I find out what you've done with the necklace,' he told her with uncompromising decision. His implacable eyes kindled, and she realised with a cold clenching of her heart that he meant it.

Dry-mouthed, she protested, 'That's kidnapping.'

'You can go as soon as the necklace is in my hands.'

She cast him a glance of mingled shock and distrust. 'I don't imagine your cousin would be happy to learn that you're holding me prisoner.'

His expression darkened, but he said coolly, 'I'll worry about Alex if and when I have to.'

'You're being completely crazy!' She tried to infuse her voice with crisp scorn. 'And I'm not going to put up with it. Your ancestors might have been able to shut up anyone who offended them in the dungeons, but this is a different world.'

Back held so stiffly she thought she could feel her spine cracking, she swung on her heel and set off for the door. She'd only taken two steps when he stopped her with a hand on her upper arm, one smooth, decisive movement swinging her around to face him.

Every treacherous sense quivered at the faint, intensely masculine scent that was solely his, an evocative sexual promise that set her heart racing. Her stomach clenched as she shivered at the electricity that poured through her, destroying defences she'd been so sure would never be breached again.

In a cracked voice she muttered, 'Gabe, be sensible! You can't do this!'

'Who's going to stop me? You?' His smile was a masterpiece of cold irony.

Before she could formulate an answer he bent his head and kissed her, his mouth demanding the response she dared not give. But although she could keep her lips clamped tightly together, she couldn't control the spontaneous, involuntary betrayal of her body.

Of course he understood each sensual signal. He knew her too well not to recognise the quickening pulse-rate, the heat that stung her lips and skin, the bemused, sultry droop of long lashes over dazed green eyes as she fought her reckless surrender.

And his body reciprocated with fierce awareness, a forceful tension that sent more electricity sizzling through her. Whatever he thought of her, believed her to be, he wasn't immune to the dangerous primal chemistry that raged between them.

The kiss hardened into urgency, and her willpower snapped. On a muffled groan she lifted her arms and reached for him, desperate to enjoy for a few seconds more that sense of utter security she'd always felt when he'd held her, as though nothing and nobody could ever hurt her again.

He pulled her into the powerful planes and angles of his big, lithe body, imprinting her with his need while his mouth plundered hers in a blaze of carnal pleasure.

For a few precious moments she let herself savour the potent sensation of her breasts crushed against him, the strong arm that held her hips clamped to his. And then he lifted his head.

Muttering something in a harsh, jagged voice, he dropped his arms and stepped back, a slash of colour along his barbaric cheekbones contrasting with the ice-blue of his narrowed eyes.

He'd spoken in Illyrian, but the words and tone didn't need any translation. Swallowing to ease her dry throat, she said hoarsely, 'I couldn't agree more. Not one of your better ideas.' Although her lips felt tender, and her body throbbed with unappeased need, she met his eyes defiantly. 'What were you trying to prove?'

'Don't push your luck,' he said roughly. 'You have no power here, Sara.'

She shrugged and turned blindly away, only to trip over the edge of a chair. Instantly he caught her by the arm.

'Are you all right?' She didn't answer, and his grip tightened to give her a slight shake. 'Answer me, Sara.'

When she winced theatrically he loosened his grip, but didn't let her go. Adrenalin pumped through her and her muscles tightened as she weighed up her chances of getting away if she kneed him in the groin or clawed at his eyes.

A metallic gleam in his eyes warned her that he knew what she was thinking. In spite of her fitness she had no hope of matching his lean, virile strength.

'Try it,' he invited softly. 'Try me, Sara.'

His words ricocheted around her brain, momentarily silencing her. Mesmerised, she stared at him while time stretched; she could sense his readiness, his formidable confidence. Tension hummed like electricity between them, taut with unspoken hunger.

She had to get out of this! She searched for words, but when they came they were thin and ineffectual. 'You tried me, Gabe, and condemned me without a hearing.'

'I heard a pack of lies,' he said indifferently. 'Try me with the truth.'

She closed her eyes, then forced them open to glare at him. 'You wouldn't accept the truth if it hit you in the face! Eventually you'll have to let me go.'

'Why?'

When she stared at him he lifted a black brow and smiled.

'Who would miss you?' he asked, in a voice that sent chills scudding the length of her spine.

'Don't be so stupid! Of course I'd be missed! I have friends….' She lifted her chin and met his implacable gaze, pitiless and unforgiving as Arctic seas. 'Besides, you don't want me here.'

'I think I've just shown why I might want you here, always ready, always waiting for me.'

Shock almost robbed her of speech. He was toying with her, she thought valiantly, cruelly manipulating her with his implied threats.

'Then you'll have to kill me eventually, because when you let me go the first thing I'll do is go to the police. And if the police here are so delighted to have their wolf back that they refuse to do anything about it, I'll contact Interpol. And the press.'

'Would anyone believe you if you tried to lay charges?' he asked, burnished eyes opaque and unreadable. 'No one knows why our engagement was broken; if anyone gets wind of your presence here, they'll assume we're trying again. Everyone loves a fairy story, and our engagement had all the right ingredients.'

The fingers on her arm relaxed, slid down to grip her elbow; he urged her across the room, releasing her only to hand back the glass of champagne she'd abandoned.

Sara clutched the glass as though her life depended on it. Hoarsely, she said, 'This is the twenty-first century and you're a modern man, not some medieval despot who can get away with murder.'

'I don't plan to murder you,' he said with insulting patience. 'I intend convincing you that your freedom depends on telling me where the necklace is. Once you've done that you can go.' His mouth compressed into a straight line. 'And you'll be rich enough to do what you want, provided you keep out of my way.'

He still had the power to hurt her so badly she could barely breathe. Goaded into defiant indiscretion, she hurled back, 'I can't think of anything I'd enjoy more. But I don't *know* where the wretched necklace is!'

And had to cope with another of those killer silences, seething with unspoken thoughts and hidden emotions.

When he finally spoke it was with a slight sardonic twist to his beautiful mouth. 'Of course, if money doesn't work there are always other ways to find out.'

Other ways? One glance at the smouldering depths of his eyes told her what he meant. Now he knew that he could use their potent mutual attraction to seduce her.

And he would, she thought, sickened and horrified. He hated her, but he'd make love to her because he wanted to find the necklace so badly.

Sara panicked. Without thinking, she flung the contents of her glass into his face.

The champagne broke against the granite angles of his face. Appalled at her stupidity, she watched him wipe the liquid away with a handkerchief.

On a broken little gasp she muttered, 'Oh, hell, I'm sorry,' and set her glass down.

Gabe balled up his handkerchief and threw it into the grate. Dispassionately he watched it burn, then smiled, and her heart shuddered.

'It amuses me, the contrast between your elegant, composed face and that passionate, sensuous mouth,' he said urbanely, his perfect control of English subtly affected so that the sentence had an alien intonation. 'You look every inch an aristocrat—serene, well-bred, completely in control—and I liked knowing that in my arms, in my bed, you turned into a wildcat—reckless and sexy and elemental.'

Stunned by his words, she stared into his face. Their eyes clashed in primeval combat. Gabe smiled, his dark face compelling in its vengeful strength, and came towards her. Sara's breath stopped in her throat as she tried to struggle free of the dark spell he'd always been able to cast.

But she left it too late. Even as she twisted to run, his hands closed over her shoulders, and he pulled her into his aroused body.

Heat engulfed her—heat and fire and an untamed, erotic craving that terrified her.

'It's still there, damn you,' he said between his teeth, and he lowered his head and kissed her again.

And she fought him again, furious at her body's betrayal of her mind and her heart, until the unsparing mastery of his lips summoned a reckless need that consumed everything else in its clamour for satisfaction.

He slid one hand up behind her head, strong fingers working smoothly against her sensitive scalp as he gentled the kiss, and she sighed into his mouth, shivering with pleasure. The smooth touch of his fingers on the back of her head sent arrows of intense delight through every cell in her body; too late, she realised that he was loosening the pins that held her sleek chignon in place. Her hair fell in a warm, heavy mass around her neck and shoulders, adding a sensuous friction to the explosions along her nerves already caused by his addictive mouth and deft hands.

He moved slightly, accommodating her eager body in the cradle of his hips. The appetite he'd unleashed in her increased exponentially at the hard evidence of his arousal. She had to grit her teeth and jerk her head away to stop herself from pressing against him and giving up on the futile struggle to keep her sanity.

Each kiss, each caress, was an exercise in power, she thought frantically: he was showing her how easily he could have her.

Desperately she gasped, 'No!'

CHAPTER FOUR

THE shifting, flexing muscles in Gabe's torso and arms locked into stasis.

Sara looked up into blue eyes glittering with lust and saw him reimpose control with an effortless ease that was like a blow to the heart.

Yes, he'd been testing her.

She forced words between her lips, wincing when she heard her voice, husky and rough with a longing she couldn't hide. 'You don't have to pretend that you want me, Gabe. I don't have any information to give you, so this seduction routine isn't going to achieve anything.'

'Beyond using up surplus energy?' he said brutally, but he released her, turning away as though her violent, unwilling response had sickened him.

As it probably had.

It had certainly sickened her. She looked down at her trembling hands and said tonelessly, 'I've had enough. I'm leaving right now.'

'You're not going anywhere.'

Sara marshalled words in her mind, words that might convince him that this was an exercise in futility—and a dangerous exercise at that. Her surrender had been humiliating enough, but what really frightened her was that he'd wanted her almost as much as she'd wanted him. His belief that she'd stolen the ruby necklace should have killed that wildfire hunger completely.

She hated being so vulnerable!

Oh, she was entirely safe from falling in love with him again. Once was enough, she thought bitterly.

But wanting him—that was an entirely different matter.

Even when she'd believed that he'd loved her, the intensity of passion had alarmed her; it had felt like handing her whole self over to him.

Numbly she blurted, 'If I were a thief I'd have taken the money you just offered me.'

'Not if you were planning to hold out for more,' he said coolly. 'If I'd accepted that Marya had stolen the necklace, you'd have had both the money you got for selling it and an intact engagement, with eventual access to my bank account when we married. By your reckoning, you've missed out.'

'That is a foul thing to say,' she retorted, shoring up her composure with anger, only to tamp it down because it wouldn't get her anywhere. She drew in a jagged breath and tried reason. 'Gabe, holding me prisoner isn't going to work because I don't know anything about the theft. For the same reason, seducing me won't achieve anything. Acting like one of your robber baron ancestors might satisfy your need for revenge, but it won't get you what you want.'

He shrugged. 'I don't want revenge,' he said briefly, and poured more champagne into her glass, his angular, clever face reflective.

Hope warmed into life inside her. Perhaps her refusal of his insulting offer had begun to—oh, not to convince him, not yet, but make him wonder if he might be wrong about her? This whole situation was so unlike him.

Although he had a reputation for dangerous manoeuvres, his career had been marked by a keen intelligence that carefully calculated every risk.

Until they'd met. And now, this kidnapping…

'You could let me go,' she said quietly, knowing that if he did it would be another, final ending. She'd never see him again except in the newspapers and on television. 'I won't tell anyone what happened.'

His expression hardened into cynicism. 'Nothing's happened, Sara. And you can stop looking at me with those wide, scared eyes. I don't plan to torture the truth out of you, or lock you in a dungeon for the rest of your life.'

'So what do you intend to do?' she shot back.

He handed her the champagne flute, seemingly not aware of the way her breath caught in her throat when their fingers touched.

Picking up his own glass, he said abruptly, 'I'll make a deal with you. If you didn't have anything to do with stealing the Queen's Blood, you might still know something that would help—some scrap of information that doesn't seem important, something that will lead to the thieves. We'll go over what you recall, and if at the end of the week nothing comes of it then you can go.'

She crushed a spark of angry rebellion. Gabe was arrogantly playing with her life, ordering it to suit himself because she didn't have the power to prevent him. But that last offer sounded as though he was prepared to compromise.

Dared she trust him? She scanned his handsome, enigmatic face.

No way.

Yet it would soothe some yearning part of her if she could persuade him that she had nothing to do with the theft. Warily, she said, 'I don't—'

He cut her off, his expression brooking no further shilly-shallying. 'Just give me an answer, Sara.'

She said coldly, 'I have no choice, do I?'

'No.'

'I think I'd rather be a prisoner than go through the pretence of being a guest and *helping you with your enquiries*.' She loaded the phrase with sarcasm. 'At least that would be honest. But if it will convince you that I truly don't know anything, I'm game. And of course I'll work on the bedrooms as well. However, what will happen at the end of the week when I've come up with nothing?'

'You go back to your job and I won't bother you again.'

Go back to a fake career, working for a man who'd been paid to hire her? *Never*.

Steeling herself, she said, 'All right, it's a deal.'

Gabe lifted his glass with a narrow, totally confident smile that set her teeth on edge. 'Here's to prising something loose from your memory.'

She raised her champagne to her lips and sipped. It was superb, the cool liquid sliding like nectar over her tastebuds. 'Here's to the truth.'

'Indeed.' Gabe's broad shoulders moved in a shrug as mocking as his thin smile. 'I'll always drink to the truth—whatever it is, and however hard it is to accept.'

The champagne, crafted with exquisite care to enhance occasions of pleasure and delight, tasted like flat soda water. Why had Gabe chosen it?

Because he was a cynical bastard, she decided, suddenly sickened by the charade.

She put her glass down with a tiny ringing sound. 'If you don't mind, I'll ask for a tray in my room. It's been a long day and I'm tired.'

Gabe lifted a taunting eyebrow. 'But what a pity to

waste that elegant outfit. Dinner's ready now, so you might as well join me. I won't keep you up late.'

Colour flooded her skin, ebbing abruptly to leave her white and shaken by his deliberate cruelty. He'd said those same words to her often, and always it had meant that he was as eager to go to bed as she, hungry to lose himself in the glory of their lovemaking.

He knew, too, that she'd remember. But in his castle he called the shots.

Pride whipped up enough defiance to stiffen her spine. To hell with hoping he'd see that she would never have stolen from him! She'd been an idiot to think—even for a few minutes—that he might change his mind. As soon as she got back to her room she'd get on her mobile phone and organise her escape. Until then she'd play for time.

Like the study, the large dining room was panelled in mellow golden stone pine. Its windows shuttered against the night, it glowed like a benediction. A magnificent landscape on one wall caught her eye immediately; no art expert, she recognised the style of a Renaissance master. It was matched on another wall by an ancestor with Gabe's eyes and mouth and the same uncompromising aura of power. A carved chest—a splendid eighteenth-century antique, she noted with professional appreciation—showed off a collection of silverware that would have made her mouth water at any other time.

Gabe sat her down at the table and Webster, the manservant, served them with the first course, a vegetable and cheese torte that smelt divine and was accompanied by a salad of ripe tomatoes and olive oil.

Determined to stay aloof and composed, Sara observed steadily, 'What a delightful room. In spite of its size, it's almost cosy.'

As the silent servant left the room Gabe answered, 'The study and this room have both been returned to the way they were in my grandparents' time. There's another, more baronial dining hall, with a huge table that looks as though it's been there since the Dark Ages, but I was sure you'd prefer to eat here. Much more intimate.'

Her stomach knotted at the edged note in his voice, but she forced herself to nod. 'I'm glad the castle didn't suffer too much damage during the occupation.'

His expression hardened. 'Unless you count the tyrant's ideas of interior design. The castle wasn't demolished for various reasons, one of which was that he used it as a private hunting lodge.'

Something in his tone caught her attention. 'You never say his name.'

He gave her a tight, mirthless smile. 'His name was the same as mine—Considine.'

Sara's gaze flew to his face, cold and hard and grim. 'What a coincidence,' she said inanely, unable to think of anything sensible.

'No coincidence. He was a very distant cousin.'

Sara frowned. 'But—I thought he killed your grandparents.'

'There are no quarrels so vicious as family quarrels,' Gabe said lethally. 'The name he was known by is a nickname—it means wolf in Illyrian. He hunted my grandparents down like the wolf he was, torturing and killing innocent people until finally someone cracked and betrayed them. He wanted them alive, but they both died, thank God, in a hail of bullets. So he hung their bodies on gibbets in front of the walls.'

The delicious torte turned to ashes in her mouth. 'I'm so sorry.' Sickened and horrified, she had to stop herself from putting a comforting hand on his.

'War is never pretty, and a civil war is crueller than any other,' Gabe said grimly. 'Fortunately for the people here, his obsession with killing animals meant that he didn't clear the valley and turn it into a collective farm. Nevertheless he punished the people in the valley by deliberately denying them resources. They had no doctor, no schools, none of the amenities of modern life.'

During their whirlwind courtship and engagement they'd rarely discussed the years his country had suffered under the iron heel of the dictator. And even then Gabe had kept the conversation superficial.

So why was he telling her now?

She said, 'Where was your father when this happened?'

'Immured over winter at the South Pole.' Gabe sipped some of his wine and looked across at the portrait on the wall. 'He was a scientist with the New Zealand party there. By the time he got back to civilisation it was all over. But he never forgot Illyria or the valley. Or that he had been secure while his people were suffering.'

'No wonder the Illyrians almost forced your cousin back on the throne,' she said sombrely. 'I remember watching it on television. I thought it was the most romantic thing I'd ever seen—snatching him from the airport and driving him straight to the cathedral to crown him. It was so incredibly moving—those silent people demonstrating in the silent streets, and then the bells and the cheers and everyone weeping and calling out to him as though he'd brought them back to life.'

'He did exactly that. Alex is both pragmatic and determined. Once he'd accepted that he was needed here, he talked my brother Marco into managing his business empire, so that Alex could sink himself and his considerable assets into the task of hauling Illyria into the twenty-first century without destroying everything that makes it special.'

'From all accounts he's doing a great job. Did he persuade you to come back?'

Gabe sent her a swift glance. Did she know that he'd agreed to Alex reaffirming him as Grand Duke? His eyes flicked to the lush contours of her mouth. Satisfied with the answering green sparks in her eyes, and the wash of colour across her elegant cheekbones, he decided that she was showing no more than conventional interest, steering the conversation into a neutral topic, away from the grim reality of blood and death.

Once he'd admired her social skills, but they grated now; he wasn't accustomed to having her treat him as an acquaintance.

From the moment he'd seen her again his reactions had surprised and irritated him—an irritation that had turned into cold fury with himself when he'd lost the plot entirely and kissed her, reawakening the voracious carnal appetite he'd thought dead.

'I believed it was time the Illyrians had a chance to determine their own destiny, but Alex convinced me they need our help,' he said, silently cursing the rough timbre of his voice.

She nodded, flicked a glance at him, then let her thick, long lashes hide her eyes before lifting them to look around the room, her lovely face serene as her gaze rested on the silverware in the chest. No doubt her thief's calculator of a mind had noted on it the wolf crest the first Grand Duke had made his own, estimated its value, and realised each piece would have to be sold privately, like the Queen's Blood.

'Of course,' he said evenly, 'one of the first things I did once I took over here was to install an extremely good security system.'

A pulse at the base of her long throat throbbed, and her

fingers tightened around the stem of her wine glass when she picked it up, but she met his gaze over the rim with limpid poise.

It gave Gabe fierce, dangerous pleasure to know that her civilised mask still vanished the moment he touched her. He'd wondered if her desire had been as false as her pretended love; now he knew it wasn't. Oh, she could quite easily have faked the softening of her body, the inrush of breath, but the swift colour across her beautiful skin was a genuine reaction. And so was the sultry fullness of her lips and the glazed hunger in her eyes.

She still wanted him. That, he thought with cold satisfaction as the second course arrived, was her weak point, and he'd be stupid not to use it.

Sara watched the manservant fill her glass again; the champagne might as well have been water for all the effect it was having, but she wouldn't drink any more. She needed her wits. In spite of her stomach's rebellion, she took a small bite of the food in front of her, wondering how something that looked like a chicken and vegetable stew could taste so delicious.

Once they were alone again Gabe said coolly, 'Starving yourself isn't going to help. You're too thin as it is.'

Mixed anger and grief solidified into a hard lump in her stomach, banishing any remnant of appetite. Although she felt as brittle as the champagne glass in front of her, she managed to produce a measured, temperate response. 'I'm exactly the same weight as I was—' She suddenly realised what she'd intended to say and fumbled for something else. 'A year ago.'

When I last saw you was too personal, too filled with anguished memories. The last time she'd seen him he'd ordered her out of his presence as though she were something slimy and disgusting, refusing to listen to her shocked denials, her horror at the situation she'd so unexpectedly found herself in.

At their brief last meeting she'd discovered that beneath the handsome face and formidable sophistication of the man she'd thought she knew was another man, one whose possessive instincts had almost overwhelmed him.

He'd wanted to kill her, she thought, and panic engulfed her, shortening her breath and sending her thoughts whirling in useless fear.

She had to get away.

'You don't look it,' he said abruptly, half-closed eyes calculating as they assessed her. 'Slender is one thing—scrawny is an entirely different look.'

The insult barely registered. 'I'm fine,' she said automatically.

But the past year had altered her; some inner part of her was forever broken. It had changed him, too. His handsome face had hardened into austerity, as though the months since she'd seen him had been difficult.

Well, they probably had been; his arrogant, aristocratic pride would have been savaged by the huge media furore that had followed his decision to call off their engagement.

Not that she could blame the press for turning a private tragedy into a very public, very blatant scandal. After all, she thought, deliberately hurting herself, what could be spicier and sell more newspapers than the complete meltdown of the engagement between a high-flying billionaire with ancient aristocratic connections and a nobody from some tiny Pacific island?

The media had hounded her, staking out her small flat, dogging her footsteps with their calls for comments and the constant popping of flashbulbs in her face. In the end, worn out by grief and fear, she'd made the mistake of accepting Hawke Kennedy's offer of refuge on his country estate. He'd only spent one night there with her, but that had been enough to set off another round of hideous, suggestive rumours.

Not that Gabe had mourned for long; photographs of him with various gorgeous women had regularly hit the social pages until a few months ago, when he seemed to have settled down with one particularly clever and chic Parisienne who ran an art gallery.

Sara hid a violent stab of chagrin and jealousy by pretending to sip more wine.

'You don't look fine, you look exhausted,' he observed bluntly.

'That might have something to do with getting up at an ungodly hour to fly halfway across Europe, then being confronted by you,' she retorted, biting out each word.

White teeth gleamed in his bronze face and his eyes were amused. 'You never did like being woken up early.'

Stunned, Sara fought for breath. He had humiliated her, refused to trust her word and manipulated her life, and yet still—*still*—she had to fight back a white-hot excitement when he smiled at her. It was so totally unfair!

In spite of everything, his potent charisma burned through every defence, homing in on the passionate craving that had never gone away. Oh, their relationship had started with sex, but then their minds had seemed to mesh and she'd found they shared the same sense of humour—all leading to her growing conviction that they were soul-mates.

And to her incredulous delight he'd asked her to marry him. She'd believed heaven could offer no more…

Grief pounced, a dark pall that had been her constant companion since he'd thrown her out of his life.

'What's wrong?' he asked crisply, black brows drawing together.

Only pride gave Sara the strength to produce an offhand shrug. 'I'm sorry if I'm not being good company. I did warn you I was tired.'

'Eat up—and don't think that playing with your food is going to persuade me you've eaten it. If necessary I'll feed you myself.'

Although he met her simmering glance with a cool smile she saw the flint-hard determination beneath. A mixture of excitement and self-disgust sickened her; she lifted food to her mouth and began to chew.

Gabe made a crisp comment on the state of the local roads. From there he segued into his cousin's plans for Illyria, which led to his ideas for his own huge estates, until eventually an astonished and exasperated Sara realised that not only was she conducting a stimulating conversation with him, but that she'd also finished the food on her plate.

He didn't comment, and he didn't insist that she eat dessert, merely asking, 'Coffee?'

'No, thank you.'

After a probing survey that lasted for several seconds too long, he allowed her to get away with it. 'I'll show you to your room.'

When she opened her mouth to demur he said blandly, 'The castle can be confusing to those who don't know it. I'd hate you to get lost.'

Cheeks pink, Sara kept her expression rigidly unmoving. In other words, he knew she'd take the opportunity to explore with a view to escaping.

She bridged the uncomfortable silence by getting to her feet. Once in the hall she said, 'You'll have to excuse my lack of knowledge about castles, but are they all rabbit warrens like this?'

'If they haven't been altered in any substantial way since they were built.' He took her elbow in an automatic gesture.

Sara concentrated hard on putting one foot before the other as they walked to the lift. His fingers on her skin, his warmth and nearness, sent a tantalising cloud of awareness through her, fogging her brain so she had to force herself to listen to his words.

'The Wolf's Lair took a couple of hundred years to finish, which explains the mishmash of towers and styles. My ancestors didn't care about architectural purity or comfort—all they wanted was a strong fortress to protect the trade route through the mountains, so as each new advance in castle-building came along they incorporated it. During the Renaissance there were alterations to make the place more comfortable, but not much has been done since then.'

'Apart from a few modern conveniences,' she observed drily as the door to the lift slid open. 'When I got here I put them down to the fake American, Mrs Abbot Armitage.'

'She isn't fake,' he said levelly. 'She's the wife of an old friend.'

A very complaisant old friend, if he didn't mind his wife lying for Gabe, Sara decided, enduring another stinging pinch of jealousy.

He said, 'The plumbing was my great-great-grandfather's sole concession to the nineteenth century. As well as redecorating, my murdering predecessor put in the elevators.'

Sara shivered at the coldly ruthless note that characterised his references to the dictator. It was the same tone he'd used when he'd banished her from his life.

When the lift slowed she asked, 'You said your cousin the Prince convinced you that the Illyrians needed you. How?'

He was silent until they emerged into the corridor that led to her bedroom, and when he spoke it was in a dismissive tone. 'Alex is very persuasive.'

Sara shot him a disbelieving glance. She couldn't see anyone being able to persuade Gabe into doing something he didn't want to.

His wide shoulders moved in a slight shrug. 'Since my grandparents were killed Illyria's been frozen in a time warp, starved of almost everything a modern state needs to survive, let alone advance. The people have no history of democracy and the infrastructure is almost non-existent. In the turmoil after the dictator's death there was a very real chance of the country going bankrupt and being swallowed up by one of the neighbouring states. After Alex contacted me, I came here and asked the people in the valley what they needed most.'

Sara looked up into his hard, intelligent face. 'And they said?'

'They said they wanted a Considine back in the Wolf's Lair.' He smiled ironically. 'After that they wanted electricity, water, and decent roads. But it was clear that, in spite of my bastard relative's tyranny, they wanted some sort of connection with the family.'

Strange, but now they were enemies she was learning so much more about him!

He pushed her door open and gave her a smile that held nothing but irony. 'Goodnight, Sara. If you need anything, pull the bell-rope and someone will come.'

Was there an underlying meaning to the words? Stiffly she said, 'Goodnight.'

The door closed behind him with a heavy thunk. Shaking, Sara leaned back against its solid wood and let out a long-stifled sigh. Seeing him again had shattered her;

she felt as though she'd been dragged into a whirlpool and sucked under.

She straightened and pulled away from the door. Self-pity was all too easy; she had to ignore Gabe's humiliating kisses and his overwhelming effect on her, and work out how to get away from his castle and out of his life.

He'd said that she might remember something that would lead to whoever had stolen the jewels, but that had been too thin a story. Perhaps he intended to grill her until she made a mistake? Or, as he thought someone else might be involved, did he assume that if he pressured her enough she'd betray this suspected other person?

Her mouth twisted. In return, no doubt, for not being charged herself?

Stupidly she'd agreed to stay, because she wanted some chance to prove her innocence, but she should have refused indignantly—if not then, as soon as he'd kissed her. It had taken her a whole year to get her life back to some sort of equilibrium. Falling into his arms—into his bed, if that was what he intended—would cripple her emotionally, and she suspected that this time it would be permanent.

For her own self-respect, she had to get out of here.

Mind working furiously, she ran across the room to the armoire, and hauled out her tote bag. She'd ring—who?

Her hands stilled as the thought struck her. Who could she ring?

Many of her so-called friends had slipped away after the debacle of her failed engagement and the storm of publicity that had followed. She couldn't ask any of the few who'd remained faithful. Gabe was too powerful. He'd destroyed her career; he was ruthless enough to do the same to anyone who helped her. She didn't dare ask her friends to go against him.

Besides, who'd believe that Gabe was holding her prisoner?

Biting her lip, she scrabbled in the bag.

So who could help? Nobody, a pragmatic part of her brain told her. But there had to be someone…

Hoping fervently that there was cellphone coverage over Illyria, she groped for her tiny mobile phone. It eluded her, as it so often did.

Demanding angrily, 'Oh, *why* do they make them so small?' she dumped the contents of her bag onto the bed.

Five increasingly frantic minutes later, she stood staring down at the mess she'd made.

There was no phone—and no diary, with its invaluable list of addresses and phone numbers. And someone had removed her credit card and the few notes of local money she'd got at the airport.

Her laptop had gone.

And so had her passport.

CHAPTER FIVE

REAL fear kicked in Sara's stomach, its cold force paralysing her thoughts.

She took an unsteady step towards the door, then veered across to the charming little desk in front of one of the windows. Perhaps an over-zealous maid had transferred her laptop and the missing items from her bag to the desk drawers?

A hurried examination revealed nothing but a stack of paper and envelopes emblazoned with the rampant wolf crest. Ignoring the growing hollowness beneath her ribs, she searched the room until she found herself tipping the contents of the drawer in the bedside table onto the bed for the second time.

She dragged in a sharp, painful breath and forced herself to stop her frenzied hunting and sit on the side of the bed. Her hands shook; she clenched them together in her lap while Gabe's final words echoed with mocking clarity in her brain.

If you need anything, pull the bell-rope....

There was a remote chance—no, less than a chance, just a faint possibility—that the maid who'd unpacked might have accidentally carried off the mobile phone.

And the credit cards and money and her passport? her mind jeered. And the laptop?

To put in a safe, perhaps?

Her heart clenched and she felt sick. This was far too close to what had happened a year ago.

Nevertheless, she set her jaw and pulled on the bell-rope.

A couple of minutes later she heard a sharp snick and looked up, eyes widening when the door swung open and she met Gabe's ironic gaze. She flinched, but got to her feet to face him, trying to ignore the erratic rhythm of her heart.

'I rang for the maid,' she said coldly. He'd changed into a black shirt and trousers, the shirt open slightly at the neck to reveal a bronze throat.

Insolent amusement curled his sensuous mouth. 'The maids are all asleep,' he told her. 'And they don't speak English, anyway.'

He'd been expecting this, she realised. Intimidating and powerful, he blocked the door. Why did he have to be so *big*?

White-hot with rage, she demanded, 'Where is my passport?'

'It's safe, along with your money and mobile phone.' He scrutinised her rigid face before adding with calculated dispassion, 'And so is your laptop. You won't be needing them. Think of this as a holiday, free from the cares of earning a living.'

'You patronising bastard,' she hissed between clenched teeth.

'You conniving bitch.'

The open insult shocked her into a gasp.

One black brow lifted in irony. 'Can't take it?' he drawled. 'But, so that we don't have to repeat this scene, I should tell you that apart from Webster, the manservant, no one here speaks English. Even if they could, they wouldn't help you escape—it's the feudal thing again. Neither will Webster. He owes me his life, and *his* loyalty is unshakeable.'

Sara bit her lip. That last barb had been aimed at her, and it stung even though it was totally unfair.

He waited with mock courtesy for her to speak. When she remained stubbornly silent he finished laconically, 'You're on your own, Sara.'

Another intimidating pause set Sara's blood thundering through her body. She felt cold and hot at once, her emotions so turbulent she clamped her lips shut in case she didn't make sense.

Gabe's handsome features hardened. With a dispassionate lack of emotion, he said, 'And your door will be locked. If you care to look out of the window you'll see that it's too high for knotted sheets to reach the ground. And I did tell you, didn't I, that the first thing I did for the castle was install the latest state-of-the-art security system?'

He knew he'd told her. Yet she'd been stupid enough to hope that his willingness to contemplate the idea that she might not be guilty meant some sort of change in his attitude. Why did she set herself up for more pain?

Sara lifted her head and stared at him, willing her voice to remain steady and cool. 'So much for that calm, reasonable idea of searching for the truth.'

He looked amused. 'I never said I trusted you, Sara. And I'm surprised that you thought I could.' Something altered in the arrogant face and his smile became speculative. 'Or were you hoping for something to help you sleep?'

He came into the room, each noiseless stride proclaiming his intention. Everything about him—the hooded, dangerous look, the charged possessiveness, the uncompromising masculine awareness—warned her that he still wanted her. Pride anchored her in place while she battled to control an astonishing mixture of emotions—fury, pain, fear, and a flaring, shameless anticipation.

Because she wanted him, too.

Registering each primitive sensation with horror, she wondered what kind of sexual hold was so strong that it survived bitter betrayal and total lack of trust. Whatever it was, it had nothing to do with love.

If she gave in to this fierce, mindless hunger, she'd be forever diminished in her own eyes—and his.

He was only a step away when she managed to say hoarsely, 'No.'

He stopped, a smile curving his mouth, his narrowed eyes both mocking and reckless.

And, in spite of everything, she couldn't control a sudden surge of wild excitement.

'Sure?' The word was a blatant invitation, reminding her of maddened ecstatic moments spent in his arms.

She had to clear her throat, but she managed to mutter, 'Absolutely sure. Not now, not ever.'

'Liar.'

He traced the outline of her mouth with a lean, knowing forefinger, so lightly it feathered across her skin, setting off an inferno inside her. Every cell in her body clamoured for him. Unable to breathe, she stood like a stone, her lashes hiding her eyes, her will bent on one thing only—resistance.

Almost immediately he stopped the small, exquisite torture, and turned away as though she sickened him.

'I'll see you in the morning,' he said harshly when he reached the door.

It closed behind him and this time she heard the key turn.

Shaking, Sara collapsed onto the huge bed. *Think*, she commanded herself. You need to think….

But a yawn cracked her face. The reckless rush of adrenalin ebbed from her body, leaving her limp, her bones aching as though she'd been beaten.

Oh, why did she cave in whenever he touched her? His kisses were insulting, each one a cruel statement of power and lust, yet she responded with helpless passion.

Had he brought her here out of some need to exorcise her? Surely he didn't feel he could make love to her until he was sated with her and then just toss her away like a used washcloth?

No. He wanted the Queen's Blood, and he was certain she had it, and so he was going to use every weapon at his command to find it—and his sexual hold over her was just one of those weapons.

A glance at her watch revealed that she'd been awake for almost twenty hours.

Tomorrow, she promised, her mind clouded by exhaustion, she'd work out what to do. Right now, she'd better get some sleep.

In the bathroom, she washed her face with her own soap and cosmetics, refusing even to touch the ones Gabe had provided.

Damn this overwhelming hunger! It shamed her utterly.

With swift strokes she applied moisturiser to her face, then stared at herself in the mirror, slitting her eyes as she said softly, 'He thinks you're a lying, thieving slut with no morals. Remember that if he tries to kiss you again.'

She'd be mistress to no man. That taunting part of her brain wondered why she was so adamant now, when she'd surrendered to his overwhelming masculine charisma almost without resistance not much more than a year ago.

'Love is the difference,' she said slowly, swift, aching tears clogging her voice. She'd loved him so much….

* * *

A knock on her door woke her after a night racked by hideous dreams. Dazed, she buried her face in the pillow, until the sound of Gabe's voice brought her bolt upright.

'Good morning, Sara,' he said from the doorway, his voice textured by amusement. 'You've slept long enough.'

Her mouth dried and her heart jumped. Dressed in riding trousers that clung to his heavily muscled thighs and narrow hips, and a shirt that revealed the breadth and formidable power of his shoulders, he looked like some Mediterranean deity out of myth—magnificent, dominant and inscrutable.

'What do you want?' she croaked, totally at a disadvantage. Pushing her tangled hair back from her face she snapped, 'Get the hell out of here!'

His kindling gaze swept across the camisole that didn't hide enough of her shoulders and breasts. Involuntarily, she dragged up the sheet to shield herself, but inside she melted, caught up in a fire that had never entirely died.

She'd fallen so completely, so intensely in love with Gabe, surrendering so completely to his intense masculinity, that his lack of trust had been the utmost betrayal.

Now she knew why he'd trusted the maid above her, but it didn't make her desolation easier to bear.

'Don't worry,' he said contemptuously, 'I don't make the same mistake twice. I thought you might like to come riding with me.'

When she and Gabe had met she'd told him everything about her childhood in the tropics. He knew she'd ridden bareback along the beaches of Fala'isi, that she'd only been able to get off the island because her mother had drowned in a ferocious cyclone. Yet he'd told her nothing, she thought derisively. Last night she'd learned more about him than she had in all those dazzling, dangerous months in his arms, in his bed, thinking with incredulous delight that she'd found her soul-mate.

Her heart lifted, then steadied. 'No,' she said evenly. 'I came here to do a job, and I'll do it. That's what my employer's paying me for, and, heaven knows, this room needs redecoration.'

She glanced disparagingly around at the hideous mock-baroque furniture and fake tapestries.

'But he doesn't pay you, Sara.' His voice was cool, almost amused.

'Of course he pays me!' She stared at him indignantly. Did he think she was living off the proceeds of the Queen's Blood?

'As well as organising your job, I pay your salary,' he said calmly, eyes intent and calculating in his hard, formidable face.

Stupidly, she hadn't even thought of that. But why should she be surprised?

'As it happens,' Gabe continued, 'he's quite pleased with your work. He seems to think you have talent.'

'I'll pay you back—every penny....' She couldn't go on.

A black brow etched a query in his handsome face. 'Why?'

Groping for words, she finally managed to say dully, 'Because I won't be indebted to man who thinks I stole a priceless family heirloom two weeks after we got engaged!'

'If it's so important to you, there are other, much more pleasant ways to repay a debt,' he told her with lazy assurance, wide shoulders shrugging off her pride and disillusionment.

It took a moment or two before his meaning penetrated her dazed mind. She'd let the sheet fall, and the flimsy camisole hid nothing—and Gabe was enjoying the view. His mouth curled cynically as she automatically followed his gaze down to the two peaked breasts that signalled the heat of her emotions.

Only this was fury, not arousal.

'Get out!' she snarled, hot with shame at the insult as she hauled up the sheet again.

Dark colour highlighted the sculpted cheekbones Gabe had inherited from some marauding ancestor who'd ridden out of the East, sword in hand, loot on his mind, with genes so potent they'd marked generations of Considines.

'You don't want me to leave. Your body doesn't lie, Sara.' An ironic, humourless smile didn't soften his mouth. 'Nor does mine.' He gestured at himself.

Sara's eyes widened. Colour blazed in her cheeks as she realised that he was aroused, and deep within her a reckless surge of passionate hunger answered.

He went on coolly, 'I still find you very attractive. And, as we no longer have to go through the meaningless rituals of courtship, we can perhaps forge a more honest, equal relationship.'

She stabbed a shaking forefinger at him. 'While you believe that I stole the Queen's Blood?'

'If you can prove to me—'

Sara wanted nothing more than to sink back against the pillows and weep for hours, but stubborn pride held her upright, kept her voice unwavering, her eyes more sombre grey than glinting green. 'It's up to you to prove I did, Gabe. How can I prove I didn't? You made your choice; now you have to live with it. I'm not coming riding with you. I'm going to work up a scheme for the three bedrooms you got your friend's wife to ask for, starting with this one. That's what I'm here for and that's what I'll do.'

'I'd have thought that you'd want to explore—search for ways to get away.'

Of course she did!

'Don't try to manipulate me.' She flared, then caught

herself up. It took a huge effort of will to impose some control over her shaking voice, but she managed it. 'I'm not stupid. No doubt you've made it impossible for me to escape, and I don't go in for banging my head against a brick wall. I only hope you weren't lying when you promised to let me go at the end of a week.'

A negligent shrug was the only answer to her lie—and its challenge. 'Get up and put on clothes suitable for riding.'

Their eyes met, clashed and duelled.

Gabe finished softly, 'Or I'll do it for you.'

He meant it. And she knew where that could end—*would* end! Treacherous pulses racing, she capitulated, hoping she could trust him.

Trust? Hah. She trusted him about as much as he trusted her—not a bit.

But she did need to find out as much as she could about this place.

Gabe held all the cards in his strong tanned fingers: she was his prisoner, her boss was in his pay, and her few friends wouldn't worry if they didn't hear from her for weeks.

And he was completely convinced she'd stolen his heirloom jewels, the treasure of his house. No, he wouldn't let her go. The sophisticated tycoon who'd swept her off her feet was only a mask; beneath it lurked a ruthless throw-back to his tough medieval ancestors, the wolves of Illyria.

So she had to get herself out of here.

As he'd just pointed out, knowledge was power. The more she knew about the valley, about the castle, the better it would be when she made a break for freedom.

Heart still drumming in her ears, she eyed him with what she hoped would pass for a neutral gaze. This effortless physical response was an illusion, a nasty trick played by her hormones; it had nothing to do with love.

'All right,' she said steadily. 'I'll ride with you.'

'I'll meet you here in half an hour,' he said, although they both knew he could come and go as he pleased in her bedroom.

Without waiting for an answer he swung on his heel and headed for the door with long, silent strides.

Sara clenched a fist over her heart, willing it to slow down. Once the door had closed behind him she leapt out of bed and hurried into the bathroom.

Half an hour later Gabe knocked on her bedroom door, not surprised when she called out immediately, 'Come in.'

Sara had never kept him waiting—not for appointments, not for sex, he thought cynically. But then, when she'd studied him with a view to stealing the Queen's Blood, she'd have discovered that he disliked wasting time.

He unlocked the door and pushed it open. She was standing by the desk, staring at a sheet of paper. Every muscle in his body contracted in sudden reckless craving, but she didn't move, not even to look at him.

Although she'd chosen workaday clothes, the overall effect had been carefully judged. Navy jeans made the most of her long, elegant legs, and her boots drew more attention to her neat ankles and feet. A fine charcoal jersey outlined the lush curves of breasts and waist. She carried a jacket over her arm, and had pulled her hair back in a ponytail that emphasised her patrician features, lit by the morning light from the window.

With a grim acceptance of his weakness, he noted that her glowing skin showed no sign of foundation or powder. Instead of lipstick she relied on a sexy sheen of gloss to call attention to the soft false promise of her mouth.

He'd been certain he was fully armoured against her, but

the heady rush of hunger fuddled his brain enough to make him oddly grateful when she turned her head.

Her face closed against him, she said in a flat practical voice, 'I don't have a helmet.'

Gabe gestured to the door. 'There are several in the tack room.' And as they walked towards the elevator he said, 'Did you wear helmets when you rode along the beaches of your tropical island?'

'We always started out with them.' Her tone warming, she went on, 'Our parents were very fussy about safety, but usually we discarded the helmets along the way and collected them before we arrived back home. Fortunately, none of us ever had a bad fall.'

Outside, the air was crisp and fresh, the sky clear right to the top of the mountains. Later on, it would be hot.

Sara eyed the two grooms walking horses in a courtyard. Clearly they liked Gabe; their faces split into smiles when they saw him, smiles that turned respectful when they were transferred to her.

They didn't look as though they'd be easy to bribe….

Gabe grinned at them and said something in the local language. They both laughed, and one handed the reins of the smaller horse to him and headed back through an arched doorway in the stone wall that presumably led to the tack room.

Gabe asked, 'Do you need help to mount?'

'No, thanks,' she said shortly, and swung up into the saddle.

She expected him to let the reins go, but he didn't. So she waited, accustoming herself to the size and feel of the animal beneath her, while Gabe and the other groom talked until the second groom appeared with a helmet, which he handed with a flourish to her.

'Thank you,' she said, smiling. He nodded politely and immediately switched his attention to Gabe.

No, she thought as she put on the helmet, she'd get no help from either of these Illyrians; their body language and attitude proclaimed that they were Gabe's men through and through. How had he managed to extract such loyalty in the short time he'd been at the castle? Some of it would be traditional, but there was a real element of personal respect there, too.

So why should she be surprised? Gabe walked the earth surrounded by an aura of authority, of leadership. Most people responded instinctively to it.

And to these people he was a saviour.

Gabe handed the reins to her and walked away, mounting the bigger horse with a lithe, pantherish grace that was his alone, muscles flexing as he swung his leg over the saddle. The horse moved, and he said something to it in Illyrian, his voice deep and warm and slow. The gelding relaxed, seduced as so many women had been, Sara thought on a great surge of grief.

She touched her heels into the side of her mount and kept her wits about her as they walked through an archway in the heavy stone walls and out into the pristine day.

Even though she knew he'd never have suggested this excursion unless he was certain she couldn't escape, she'd keep her eyes open. Yet it was difficult to keep that fierce inner core of anger glowing; her heart lifted as they rode past a walled area overlooked by a small, lonely tower.

'The dovecote,' Gabe remarked when he saw her eyes flick towards it. 'The enclosure used to be the jousting ground, but it now has a swimming pool in it.'

'Did you put it there?'

'No, my grandfather did.'

She glanced up at the high, massive walls, at the blood-red creepers she'd noticed on her arrival mingling with others of a more sedate green. 'It looks impregnable.'

'It is,' he said without emphasis. 'The walls have never been breached.'

She felt as though a cloud had checked the sun's power; in his voice there was the deadly note that always came with the mention of the man who'd murdered his grandparents.

Impelled by an obscure and unnecessary need to comfort him, she said, 'The valley is lovely. No wonder your ancestors built here.'

His mouth curved. 'I doubt if its beauty had much impact on them; the castle was built to guard access to Illyria. And they didn't live here in winter—once the snow closed the pass no invading army could get through, so they retired to their much warmer estates on the coast.'

Did he own those, too?

Clearly he was a mind-reader. In a voice so dry it made her flush, he said, 'They produce grapes and fish, and there's another castle—well, a combination of villa and castle, on a cliff overlooking the sea, that needs redecorating.'

Sara nodded. They had been lovers for months, engaged for a fortnight, yet she hadn't known anything of this beyond the fact that he was related in some way to the Prince who ruled Illyria.

'Oh, this is glorious,' she said as he led the way onto a trail leading through manicured fields. Insects buzzed in the sunlight, small golden missiles darting from hedgerow to hedgerow, and the air smelled of flowers and fruit and mellow freshness.

Filling her lungs with it, she tried to ignore the reason she was there, the many and turbulent undercurrents between them, and relax. The valley stretched green and peaceful beneath the darkly forested flanks of the foothills. Beyond them loomed the peaks of the ranges, glittering white in the sun, as distant and dangerous as the man who ruled this lovely domain.

In one of the fields a man stood up from inspecting the internal regions of a small, ancient tractor that seemed held together by string and prayers. He beamed and saluted.

Sara waved, and Gabe called something that made the farmer grin and shout back a pleasantry. Gabe laughed and they went on, the small incident leaving Sara thoughtful.

How could he be so approachable to everyone else, yet so utterly uncompromising with her?

Gabe noticed, of course; he thought savagely that he'd always noticed everything about her—from her softly sensuous mouth to the straight line of her spine beneath the sweater that clung so affectionately to her slender torso. He'd once told her she looked more like an aristocrat than most born into the upper classes, and she'd pulled a face at him and said that wasn't a compliment. She wanted to look like a gypsy, passionate and free and sexy.

A couple of weeks later she'd seduced him wearing only a tiara she'd found in a bridal shop. The delicate, airy thing had been made of silver wire and set with green and gold semiprecious stones that had turned her eyes into jewels.

Gabe's body tightened as he remembered what had followed. Until then he'd always been gentle and tender with her, but that night his disciplined control had shattered, and between them they'd soared to an ecstasy that he'd never experienced before, a plane of existence that had been unbearably, desperately stimulating.

All lies, he thought savagely. As big a lie as her love, as her refusal to let him buy anything for her—all carefully plotted to make him believe she was something rare and precious in his life.

The gelding whickered, but settled when he patted its glossy shoulder.

'Where are we going?' Sara's voice was taut, as though she too had picked up the current of his thoughts.

'Up to where the Queen's Blood was first found,' he said curtly. And where it had been kept hidden by Marya for forty years.

Sara looked up at him, saw the inflexible purpose in his arrogant features, and clamped down on her automatic objection. 'Why?'

He shrugged. 'Why not? It's an interesting part of the valley's history. This is the old track through the pass. In medieval times it would have been thronged with people—pedlars, wandering friars, beggars, bards, troops of knights and their attendants, the occasional rich woman in a litter—all trying to get through the pass before the snows cut off communication.'

She looked about, thinking for a moment that she caught a glimpse of the hurrying crowd. 'And now there's nobody but us.'

Only the flying insects, a bird calling 'Who? Who? Who?' on a querulous note, and two people who once had loved each other enough to decide to marry.

Doggedly, she kept her gaze between her mount's ears, subconsciously noting that they were approaching a small village. She had loved him so much—she had damned near worshipped him, she thought with bittersweet irony. He had given her the moon and the stars—he had seen something in her that no one else had—and she had been glorified by his love, his passion, his attention.

She'd been so sure she'd found the one man in the world

who made her whole. He had introduced her to a world of the senses she'd never really believed in, a world where everything else faded into the shadows, a world where the only thing was Gabe and his love.

Only it hadn't been love.

When he spoke again she had to force herself out of that bleak world of grief and loss and intense loneliness to concentrate on his words.

'The road and rail tunnel on the other side of the valley takes all the traffic now, but it needs urgent repairs to make it safe. Like everything else in Illyria, it's run down and on the brink of collapse.'

Sara nodded blindly, pretending to look around as they came up to the honey-coloured village dozing in the sun. Nothing stirred in the street, nobody came out at the clip-clop of the horses' hooves. Perhaps it had been abandoned.

She was admiring a church perched on the top of a small hillock outside the cluster of houses when a lean black dog burst from behind a tumbledown wall and dashed across the road in front of them. Sara's mount snorted and danced backwards, but it was the precipitate arrival of a small child, skirts flapping as she brandished a stick, that really set the mare off.

Neighing, front legs flailing, the mare reared to avoid the tiny intruder. The muscles in Sara's shoulders tightened painfully as she dragged the horse's head around, praying the iron-shod hooves would miss the terrified child.

CHAPTER SIX

FROM behind, Sara heard Gabe talk, his voice a slow, slurred mixture of sounds that somehow soothed the animal until he was able to lean down and grab the reins above the mare's muzzle. His iron strength held the horse steady, giving Sara time to hurl herself out of the saddle and onto the ground.

She crouched between the cowering child and the frightened animal, hugely relieved at the lusty screams that split the air. If the toddler could yell that loudly she wasn't badly hurt.

Dimly she heard voices as she patted the little girl—no older than three, she thought disjointedly—all over. No broken bones, thank God.

'Hush, darling,' she crooned, pushing black hair back from the scarlet little face. 'Shh, shh, my pretty one. You're all right. There, there—ah, see, here's Mama.'

Scrambling to her feet, she lifted the child. At the sight of her mother, the screams stopped.

For a moment no one spoke; there was something in the air Sara couldn't understand, like the shared knowledge of a hidden mystery. And then the child began to sob again. The mother burst into tears, grabbing Sara's hand and kissing it, and saying the same words over and over again.

Everyone began talking at once. Astonished, Sara looked around to see about ten people who'd appeared out of nowhere.

Gabe's voice cut through the rising babble, the note of effortless authority silencing everyone as he dismounted and handed the reins over to a young man who expertly tethered both horses to a hitching post. The sight of that well-used post told Sara as nothing else had just how dependent these people were on the technology of their forefathers.

The child's mother turned eagerly and gratefully to Gabe, words falling from her lips. He apparently asked after the tot's welfare, and she showed him that there wasn't a mark on her daughter, finally setting her down on the ground where the little girl clung to her mother's skirt and watched Sara with her huge dark eyes.

Within five minutes everyone was laughing, and the toddler was being passed from loving arms to loving arms as the family reassured themselves she was all right. An elderly man, almost toothless but beaming, eventually plonked the child, happy now, in spite of the tearstains on her cheeks, into Gabe's arms.

To Sara's amazement, his expression softened into tenderness. Smiling down into the slightly worried little face, he dropped a kiss on her forehead.

'She is like a rose,' he said, turning to Sara after he'd handed her to her mother. 'They want to thank you for saving their little one.'

Unevenly, Sara said, 'You saved her. I damn near killed her!'

'Your swift reactions and strength turned the mare. And when I looked down you were shielding the child with your body,' he said brusquely. 'That's what the mother saw, too. Are you all right?'

'I'm fine.' Oddly touched by the curt enquiry, she spread out her hands. 'Not a thing wrong with me.'

His eyes narrowed. 'You've cut your fingers,' he said, in an oddly tense voice.

Flushing, acutely aware that everyone was watching and listening, Sara closed her fingers over the smarting weal made by the reins. 'Not really.'

Someone appeared with a bottle and some tumblers, and before she realised what was happening Sara had been given one filled with white wine and the child's father was making a speech, clearly alluding to her and Gabe in the most laudatory of terms. She blinked, keeping her eyes studiously on the tumbler of wine, while a bubble of something perilously close to hysteria filled her chest. Surely they didn't expect her to drink this on an empty stomach?

'Smile,' Gabe ordered beneath his breath. 'And when they drink, drink with them.'

The toasts were earnest and honestly meant—and long. Sara sipped the wine and listened to Gabe's voice as he made his reply, feeling conspicuous and uneasy at the proprietary tone of his voice when he said her name. The glance he gave her—possessive, territorial—sent hot little thrills through her. He was, she thought feverishly, staking a claim.

But why?

Even more unsettling was the way the villagers looked at her—benign, almost knowing and oddly satisfied—as though they knew something she didn't.

Slowly she sipped at each toast, until the wine was gone and she felt distinctly light-headed, and nothing really seemed to matter any more.

Once the village and the effusive thanks were behind them, she said, 'What was going on there?'

Gabe's brows lifted. 'I'm not sure I understand you,' he said, his voice bland.

She winced when the rein slid across her palm and he pulled his mount up. 'You said it wasn't painful. We'll go back to the castle.'

'It doesn't need dressing; the skin's not broken. And I don't want to go back.' She gave him a tight smile, because she'd just realised what he'd been up to in the village.

Staking a claim? Indeed. And not one of the villagers would dream of helping her leave the country if she managed to escape from the castle.

Without trying to hide the sting in her words, she finished, 'And I'm enjoying this freedom.'

He reined in his horse and leaned over to stop hers with his hand on the rein. 'Get down.'

'Why?'

'I'll tie my handkerchief around it.' When she stared at him he said impatiently, 'Don't be silly, Sara. The handkerchief is clean and it will protect your palm. And it will be easier to do that if we're not still on horseback.'

His tone didn't admit of any refusal. And her hand did smart. Reluctantly accepting that cutting off her nose to spite her face was stupid, Sara dismounted.

Gabe hauled a handkerchief from his pocket. 'Give me your hand,' he commanded.

She didn't want him to minister to her. He'd already done huge damage to the barricades around her heart with his behaviour in the village, and she was afraid her defences might crumble further.

Her only safeguard lay in reminding herself that he was a ruthless, overbearing plutocrat. Setting her jaw, she held out her hand. The chafed area where the reins had sawed into her palm stood out red; he said something under his breath.

Sara froze, listening to her heartbeat pick up speed.

The tips of Gabe's lean fingers touched the fragile blue veins at her wrist, measuring that betraying pulse. He looked up sharply, his eyes fiercely gleaming, and tension crackled in the air between them, so potent it drowned out the frantic urging of her brain to get the hell out of there.

As though compelled, he lifted her hand and kissed the palm, his lips lingering, draining the soreness from the skin, setting fire to the reckless craving she tried so hard to keep secret.

Forbidden anticipation glittered mockingly through her, and she had to force her voice into action, saying with rasping intensity, 'Kisses don't heal skin, Gabe. Not unless they're between mother and child. Give me your handkerchief; I'll make a pad for it myself. And then we'll go back to the castle.'

He acknowledged her words with a taunting smile and released her. Misery building, she saw him reimpose the mask of control, leashing and effortlessly banishing the passion that had flamed between them only a moment previously.

Could anything make him lose that cool, disciplined self-possession?

Deftly, he placed the pad of cloth over her palm and bound it with another handkerchief.

'Two handkerchiefs?' she said, hiding heartbreak with lilting mockery.

'My mother believed in overkill,' he explained, his tone matching hers. He gave her back her hand and watched as she turned away and mounted again. 'How's that?'

'Much better,' she acknowledged stiffly. 'Thank you.'

Gabe swung back onto the gelding and urged it into action. 'We'll go on.' He sent an oblique glance at Sara's mutinous face. 'It's not far.'

He didn't have to tell her that any decisions would be made by him; she understood her powerlessness. Gabe might still be attracted to her, but his iron will kept his inconvenient sexual drive under merciless restraint.

Sara was not so lucky or so tough. As the mare walked sedately up the side of the mountain she reflected that she hadn't ever been able to cage her response to him. After the first glance she'd been so lost in the unfamiliar realm of desperate physical longing that she'd surrendered any hope of freedom. If he'd ignored her it might have died, as such mindless infatuations usually did, but he'd seemed just as stunned and aware of her as she had been of him.

A childhood friend had invited her to a party in London; it had been classic stuff, she thought now, a real eyes-across-a-crowded-room moment! She'd been acutely aware of his interest, even though she couldn't see who was watching her. Eventually she'd turned around to stare indignantly at him—and met eyes alight with purpose. Hard eyes that had promised her forbidden pleasure and stripped away the sophisticated veneer she was trying to keep intact.

Well, he'd more than delivered on the forbidden pleasure. Their lovemaking had been incandescent, a wild mingling that had stunned her almost as much as it had excited her. She'd had no idea that she could need so much—or that she'd be able to give as much as she took.

And even as her breath came softly through her parted lips, and her eyes turned smoky at memories of past erotic release, she reminded herself of its shallowness and her eventual disillusion.

The trees pressed closer to the narrow, ancient trail, in some spots overhanging it. Sara looked around uneasily, half expecting dreadful old apparitions to lurk in the sombre depths. No birds sang, no butterflies flitted through the green gloom, no small scuffles in the undergrowth signalled the secret life around her.

'Not far now,' Gabe said. He inspected her face. 'All right?'

'Yes, of course.' But the atavistic fear disturbed her modern sensibilities.

He gave her another searching survey. 'Then what's making you tense?'

'Nothing,' she snapped, adding with a shrug, 'Well, nothing new.'

To her surprise, he grinned, warming her heart into foolish pleasure. 'We'll have something to eat and drink when we get there.'

There was a dell, a smooth cup of grass in the trees, one side open to the valley. In the middle, a huge stone thrust upward, its rough grey sides oddly marked, as though aeons ago someone with primitive tools had tried to shape it. A small trickle of water emerged from the forest and lapped around the base of the stone, its sound thin and surreptitious in the silence, before it tumbled towards the cliff edge and hurled itself over.

Unlike the close-hung trees over the trail, this didn't feel ominous; it seemed expectant, waiting for something that might never happen.

Sara shivered, and her horse jibbed, jerking her head anxiously.

'What is this?' she asked hoarsely.

Gabe gave her a considering glance. 'A menhir. It's a glacial rock that was dragged here several thousand years ago and set up to mark something—a boundary, perhaps, or the way to the pass.'

'Or a site for sacrifice,' she said sombrely, trying to ignore the tightening of her skin.

'Possibly,' he agreed, irony overlaying the word.

Had she sounded like someone out to get a cheap thrill? She slid down from the mare, saying prosaically, 'Where shall I tether her?'

Already down, Gabe took a pack from behind his saddle and handed it to her. 'There's a pool against the cliff-face through the trees. I can tether them there. Take out the rug from the pack and choose a place to picnic.'

With resentful eyes she watched him lead the two horses away. He looked completely at home here, broad of shoulder and lean-hipped, long legs striding confidently into the shadowy space beneath the trees. A stray beam of sunlight kindled blue flames from his black hair, and her heart turned over.

She'd thought she was over him, but that first glance at the castle had proved her utterly wrong. Left alone, she might eventually be able to chisel him from her heart, but he wasn't going to leave her alone, and she couldn't prove that she didn't have the Queen's Blood.

If only she could convince him to check up on Marya….

But why would the woman who had risked so much to protect the jewels steal them from the man she'd saved them for? Gabe was right—it simply didn't make sense.

Sara was still standing there, the pack in her hands, staring at the menhir, when Gabe came back. He saw her brace herself and turn, her pale face carefully blank.

'So this is where the Queen's Blood was found. Did your grandfather hide it here?' she said evenly, eyes too steady.

He took the pack from her, every instinct on full alert. He'd brought her here hoping to shake those prickly defences of hers, but this was more than he'd expected.

'Come over here and we'll sit down.' She followed him obediently and he undid the pack. 'The treasure was originally found here, but my grandfather thought it was too obvious a hiding place so he hid it in the castle.' He shook out a rug and gestured for her to sit down, waiting until she'd done so before asking, 'Does your hand hurt?'

'No,' she said vaguely, not even looking at it. She swallowed, then said with obvious effort, 'If I'm a bit wan it's probably because my head is definitely feeling the effects of a full glass of wine on an empty stomach.'

He had to give her credit for an attempt at her usual spirited attitude. 'And probably the adrenalin rush from rescuing the child is fading fast. We can deal with that right now.'

Sara had to force herself to eat the fruit and yoghurt he unpacked, but her appetite soon perked up and she was able to demolish a slice of crusty bread and butter with delicate greed. 'Mmm, that was delicious.'

'Pour some coffee for yourself, and for me, too.' He handed a vacuum flask to her.

The intimacy of the moment struck her with poignant, bittersweet intensity. She'd poured coffee for him at breakfast so often, sometimes in bed, sometimes not, and she'd always cherished that small service.

Now her fingers trembled, but she managed to get the liquid into the cup and set it in front of him. 'Tell me about the Queen's Blood,' she said. 'I know that one of your ancestors found it around the twelfth century. Here?'

He leaned back against a tree trunk and surveyed her with burnished blue eyes. 'That's the accepted story. The local peasants have a different one.'

'Really?' Sara copied him, leaning against the comfortable trunk, using her cup as a shield for her face while she sipped.

'They say that once a queen came through the mountains. A beautiful woman whose dowry was the necklace, an ancient heirloom of her house. She was to marry the Emperor—'

'What emperor?' she asked.

His wide shoulders lifted. 'Who knows? She never got to him. Her party was ambushed and everyone was slaughtered. The robbers wanted to hold her for ransom, but their leader killed her, and her blood stained the menhir and hid the necklace. When the robbers searched for it, they couldn't find it.'

Hypnotised by the story, Sara said, 'Were the robbers your ancestors?'

'This took place long before the original Considine came through the pass. The peasants say that as she died the Queen was transformed into a—' He paused, then said a word in Illyrian.

'A vampire?' Sara asked, lost in the story. 'Or a ghost?'

His beautiful mouth curved. 'Neither. I think the nearest equivalent in English is the word sprite. She appeared as a beautiful woman, dangerous and secretive, who protected her hoard by luring any who searched for it to their deaths in the forest.'

Sara shivered again. It took a real effort of will to say lightly, 'I'm sure the brothers Grimm heard this tale somewhere.'

'Possibly, but even now you won't find anyone from the valley here after dark.'

Sara shivered. 'I don't blame them.'

He looked at her keenly. 'Does the place scare you?'

She took a moment to sort through her emotions. 'No,' she said slowly. 'Not scare, exactly, but I feel that it's waiting for something.' And, because she didn't want to think too much about it, she asked, 'So when did the first Considine arrive here?'

He set his coffee cup down and looked across at the huge stone. 'Around the twelfth century. Some say he was Greek, but all agree he was poor, although various ballads describe him as beautiful and kingly and deadly with a sword.'

'As ancient ballads do,' she said ironically. 'Presumably because they were composed to laud winners, not losers.'

'I'd agree. He and his band of mercenaries were coming through the pass on their way to the coast when the sprite appeared to him.' Gabe's voice grew very dry. 'It appears she'd been waiting for him down the centuries, because she offered him the Queen's Blood if he would marry her and make the valley secure from the brigands who were ravaging it.'

'If she was still beautiful I bet he agreed, even if she was a ghost,' Sara said cynically, trying to shake off the spell the story was casting. She felt as though she'd strayed into another time and place, as though the ties that bound her to the twenty-first century were weakening.

'Ah, but she appeared to him as an old hag,' he said with a sardonic smile. 'However, he was nothing if not resourceful, and he instantly saw that this bargain offered a life that promised much better pickings than that of a roving mercenary. So he took the jewels and used them as security to build the castle.'

He smiled when she demanded, 'What happened then?'

'Oh, they were married, and on their wedding night she revealed herself to him in her true form,' he said smoothly. 'Some tests of love came into it, but of course they lived happily ever after.'

Outraged, she stared at him. 'Is that all?'

'Basically. There was a lot of fighting before they got rid of the brigands, and then they had several strapping sons and set up a dynasty. Eventually one of their descendants became Prince of Illyria.'

'So why did the Queen's Blood stay here, in the valley?

It's so magnificent I'd have thought it would be removed to the capital when that happened.'

'Ah, that's the thing,' he said, watching her with an intentness that unnerved her. 'The first Considine promised his wife that the Queen's Blood would never leave the valley permanently. My ancestors were arrogant and tough, but you don't argue with a dangerous sprite—even if she happens to be your grandmother, however many times removed. The Queen's Blood stayed in the Wolf's Lair.'

Sara swallowed the last of her coffee. It tasted bitter, as bitter as her emotions. 'I wish you'd never given it to me to wear,' she said passionately.

Perhaps it was the story, perhaps her strained nerves, perhaps just a desperate need to convince him, but she did something she'd vowed never to do. Leaning forward, she touched his hand. He didn't move, but she felt his awareness beat against her, the sheer force of his will intimidating in itself.

She looked up into the dark, charismatic face, autocratic and formidable, and said urgently, 'Gabe, I swear to you that I had nothing to do with the theft of the rubies.'

Even as she spoke she knew it wasn't going to work.

His face hardened even further and he shook off her hand with a single contemptuous gesture that shattered her composure.

'Marya's father was the only person who knew where my grandfather hid the Queen's Blood,' he said harshly. 'Once the dictator took over the Wolf's Lair he had this whole place dug over—he even tried to blow up the menhir, and only stopped when he was forced to realise that no one had buried anything near it. Then my grandparents were killed and Marya's father was captured. He'd told Marya where the necklace was, so at great danger to her life she got into the castle, removed it, and buried it in her family's cow byre. And there it stayed until the tyrant was dead. Then she contacted me and took me to it. Why the hell would she steal it?'

He got to his feet in one smooth, powerful movement and looked down at her, his contempt so plain she shrank back. 'My ancestor married ugliness and found beauty,' he said in a voice that iced through her veins. 'I thought I'd found beauty in you. At least the theft of the Queen's Blood showed me that it was only skin deep.'

Sara flinched at the steely note of self-derision in his words, but scrambled up, eyes flashing and cheeks flaming. 'I didn't steal it,' she said, hot with defiance. 'You can do everything, wield your power and money like clubs, but you can't get from me what I don't have. I don't know what happened; it certainly doesn't seem that Marya would steal the gems.'

'She didn't.'

She said hopelessly, 'Has it ever occurred to you that I didn't need to steal them? That if I'd married you I would have had them for as long as I lived?'

'Oh, yes. It's also occurred to me that to stay married to me you'd have had to be faithful. I assume you realized—unfortunately just a little too late—that that was too much of a sacrifice for you to make.'

The words hit her like hailstones out of a summer sky, cold and implacable and utterly unexpected. But then, she'd made love with him only a week after meeting him. Perhaps he thought she was like that with every man she'd gone out with.

'You never really knew me, did you?' she said unevenly. 'Not that it matters.'

'Not that it matters,' he agreed, his relentless tone matched by the severity of his expression.

So hurt she couldn't see straight, she swivelled away to hide her tears, only to blunder into the little rivulet and gasp as she tripped on a turning stone.

From behind she heard a muttered imprecation, and then Gabe caught her, one arm beneath her breasts, one around her waist, and hauled her upright against his aroused body.

She gasped again, and tried frantically to pull away, but he turned her in the tight circle of his arms and she looked up into a face set in lines of savage determination, into eyes that glittered with desire.

Gabe didn't say anything; his mouth took hers, and she opened her lips to his urgent invasion, a white-hot relief beating up through her. All it took was one kiss and she was lost again….

He lifted his head, but only to say her name in a desperate, goaded voice before he kissed her once more, as though he was starving for her, as though it had been a long, heart-weary year for him, too.

As though he needed her as much as she needed him.

Dimly, she thought of resistance, but the thought faded when he invaded her mouth, making himself master of her responses. Crushed against his hard, addictive body, she surrendered to the hunger that clamoured through her. Every sense vital and keen, her cells singing with delicious pleasure, she came alive again.

He slid a hand up beneath her jersey. His long fingers closed over her breast and wildfire rioted through her, burning away every conscious thought but the need to lose herself in this drugged excitement.

Strong teeth found the delicate lobe of one ear and gently savaged it, sending shudders of anticipation through her. She turned her face into his throat and ran her hands beneath his shirt, fingertips tingling when she smoothed over the heated, burnished skin, finding the pattern of hair across his chest, spreading her palm over the driving force of his heart.

Humiliating though her complete capitulation was, she could no more deny him—or herself—what was coming than she could lie to him.

He kissed her throat, then lifted her. Somehow, between his arms and the rug, he managed to free her of her sweater and the thin shirt she wore beneath it, leaving her torso bare except for the plain bra she'd donned that morning. Hot eyes took in her dazed face as he carefully pulled her hair-tie off. Gently he picked up a handful of silken mahogany hair, then let it float onto her bare shoulders. A rough sound from his throat tore at her heart.

'You are so damned beautiful,' he said harshly. 'Like a drug in my veins, irresistible and consuming and mindless.'

She pulled at a button on his shirt. Gabe kissed her again, and when at last he lifted his head she'd opened his shirt down the front.

'I prefer you in silk and lace,' he said, his voice deep, 'but you make even that schoolgirlish bra look sexy.'

And he bent and clamped his mouth around a peaking, prominent nipple, suckling her urgently through the thin material.

Sara gave a gasping, incoherent sob and arched into his mouth, her body flexible as a bow, hands clenched against his chest while he ravished her soul from her body. Incredulously, she felt her release shatter within her, abruptly sending her over the border into that mysterious, erotic place where all that mattered was Gabe….

'You *are* hungry,' he murmured, and turned her limp body so that he could unclasp her bra.

Repelled by his blatant satisfaction, she opened her eyes. But the scornful words died when she saw his face. He could no more deny this primal craving than she could; resent it they both might, but they were trapped in this habit-forming web of passionate need.

And then he ran a lean forefinger down her breast, teasing her with the lightest of touches and stopping just short of the pleading centre, and she knew that for her this love wasn't going away.

Perhaps if she showed him how much she loved him he would understand that she could never have stolen the necklace. And even as she realised she was fooling herself, searching for reasons to placate her pride when all she wanted to do was surrender, she lifted her hands and cupped the high, magnificent sweep of his cheekbones, giving herself up completely to the heady storm of sensation.

Gabe felt her capitulation in his innermost being. He wanted to feel nothing more complicated than raw lust, but although he would have given his soul to be able to throw her on her back and take her coldly, dispassionately, he couldn't.

Her slender beauty summoned him, strong and soft and warm, skin as exquisite as magnolia petals, each curve and hollow as familiar as his own face and yet irresistibly, intensely alluring. Every muscle in his body tightened. He fought an instinctive drive to bury himself deep, deep inside her and make her his in the most primal, most inevitable way.

Relentlessly he whipped that barbaric need into submission. He bent his head to kiss her breasts, to reacquaint himself with the lush provocation of satiny skin and subtle, unmistakably female perfume.

To possess her, he thought bleakly as the sweet, sultry taste of her skin filled his mouth with delight. How the hell had such a commonplace act as making love become impossible with anyone else?

Sara had not only stolen his happiness, she'd gelded him. The knowledge burned into his pride like hot wire against his skin. His plan to seduce the whereabouts of the Queen's Blood from her had turned on him.

Perhaps he could rid himself of this demeaning obsession if he gave in to it, let himself take what she so patently offered until he was sated—until he could look at her with nothing more than a healthy man's desire for a beautiful woman. Once that happened he'd be free once more, able to call himself his own man.

He bent his head again and drew her peaked nipple into his mouth, her sudden rigidity summoning an answering surge of heat to his groin. Yes, she loved that. And he loved it that her breasts were so acutely sensitive, that she was so violently responsive to his every touch.

CHAPTER SEVEN

SARA'S pulses drummed in her ears as she stared up into eyes that promised sensual pleasure beyond belief, burning blue in Gabe's darkly dominant face. She knew that look so well.

From the first they'd barely been able to control their response to each other. Alarmed by his effect on her, Sara had refused to go out with him, tried to evade his determined pursuit.

It hadn't worked, and too soon she'd yielded to his careful wooing. Horrified by her swift capitulation to a man she instinctively knew to be dangerous, she'd been afraid that once he'd slaked his sexual hunger everything would collapse into ashes.

She'd been wrong. In spite of everything, he still wanted her.

'Gabe,' she breathed when he shifted slightly, muscles flexing beneath his bronze skin as he kissed a deliberate path to the tiny indentation of her navel.

If she let this go on she'd be lost....

Her heart was pounding so hard she could hear nothing else.

No! she thought frantically, struggling to whip up her flagging willpower. But although her lips formed the word, no sound emerged. She tried to push him away, but her disobedient hand curved around one broad shoulder, sensuously testing the strength beneath his sleek skin. Everything—common sense, self-preservation, caution—was engulfed by a feeling of such rightness that she was powerless against it.

His hand slid into her moist depths, probing slowly. Her hips jerked upwards and the last shimmers of the afterglow reignited in a powerful new flame of erotic sensation.

'Gabe…' The word emerged in a strained, raw moan.

For answer he eased his fingers further inside her.

Her nails raked across his back; past thought, she writhed against that sinfully clever hand, aware only of its shockingly potent effect on her treacherous body. 'Oh, God, *Gabe*!'

He moved onto her, thrusting into her eager, passionately receptive body with such intensity that it tore a cry from her lips.

He stopped, big body barely leashed by his will. 'Did I hurt you?' His voice was rough and his muscles tightened as he tried to draw back.

'No, you couldn't hurt me,' she muttered, and pulled herself around him, her body taut and demanding beneath him.

She locked her arms around his shoulders and kissed his throat. His powerful body tensed, but he thrust again, claiming her with a raw, primitive hunger that should have scared the wits out of her.

Instead she gloried in it.

This, she thought, barely able to formulate the words, was the real man, stripped of sophistication and worldliness, driven by a need so intense he couldn't control it.

For the first time in a year she was alive and happy, and

so keenly aware of every clamorous cell in her body that she could have wept with eager, charged anticipation.

Boldly she made him hers, driving him on as he drove her, their desire forcing them beyond the boundaries into a place where they connected with each other at the most basic, individual level.

They took and gave, they moved together in gathering ecstasy, until the building intensity took over and they reached that intangible peak together, hearts thudding, slick bodies tightly meshed in a rapturous reunion where nothing mattered but the dark, potent magic of the moment.

Later, Sara lay listening to the great tearing gasps that dragged air into her lungs. Gabe hadn't moved. Chest heaving, his lean body lay lax and heavy on her, his head still thrown back so that through her lashes she looked up into the stark, arrogant angles of his face.

Throbbing to the rapid tattoo of overloaded hearts, barely registering the faint scent of sex and sweat and desperation, she thought, *Oh, you fool!*

But her body contradicted her brain, because in some purely elemental way she had never felt so safe.

Only for a few precious seconds, until Gabe moved to lie on his back. Shivering, she made no effort to stop him. Although she wanted more than anything to hide from her stupidity, she had to accept that she'd just made the biggest mistake in her life.

Well, no, actually. Her biggest mistake had been in not running as far and as fast as she could the first time she'd met his steel-blue eyes. Except that even if she had, he'd have followed.

And that thought still had the power to fill her with a helpless satisfaction.

Sara didn't have to turn her head to check his emotions;

she could feel them, uncompromising and ominous and dangerous. It didn't help to understand that he was angry with himself because he resented this overpowering lust just as much as she did.

'Are you using contraceptives?' he asked grimly.

Shock silenced her. *Oh my God!* The words hammered through her brain, charged with such panic she didn't dare speak.

'I want the truth,' he said lethally.

Unable to lie, she hesitated before saying on a ragged breath, 'It's all right.'

'That's not an answer.'

Sara stared defiantly at his hard, purposeful face and pressed her lips together.

When Gabe said something under his breath, she flared. 'I'm not the only careless one!'

Which, of course, was a tacit admission that she hadn't even thought about contraception!

Frowning, he said shortly, 'I wasn't swearing at you,' then observed with savage self-derision, 'So much for self-control.'

And so much, he thought bleakly, for trying to get her out of his system. One look at her and, although he'd fought his surrender with every ounce of willpower he possessed, his body had taken over and done what it always wanted to do—made her his.

Why this woman? He'd had other lovers, enjoyed them for their various attributes and then said goodbye to them once the affair had run its natural course. Most were still good friends, because he chose wisely, avoiding ingenues to seek out sophisticated women who knew how these affairs should be conducted.

But he'd broken every personal rule when he'd seen

Sara, and he still couldn't understand the hold she had over him—only that her betrayal and a year apart had done nothing to ease the tormented craving that possessed him night and day.

Sara closed her eyes, unable to endure the cold contempt in his eyes. A deep, aching weariness almost pulled her under. She set her jaw and fought it, because surrendering only made things worse.

After swallowing to ease her dry throat, she said thinly, 'So what do we do now?'

Silence stretched between them, pulsing with unspoken thoughts.

Eventually he drawled, 'I'd suggest we get dressed. Not many people come this way, but it's a possibility.'

No easy answers there.

Sara sat up and stared around, bewildered by how much brighter the forest seemed, how clear and sweet the air, how sharply majestic the mountains on the other side of the valley.

Her eyes fell on the menhir. A cold whisper of air across her sensitised skin made her shudder and begin to pull on her clothes with clumsy fingers, keeping her eyes away from Gabe's lithe form as he did the same.

'I'll get the horses,' he said, and strode off into the trees.

Had he planned this scene?

Sara walked across the clearing and stood on the edge of the cliff. The ancient, unknown people who'd positioned the menhir had chosen a spot with an unobstructed view over the valley to the highest peak in the range.

No, she thought, gaze drifting across the landscape beneath, Gabe hadn't planned the wild moments in each other's arms. He despised that blazing erotic charge as much as she did.

Her tender mouth twisted. Besides, if he'd planned it

he'd have used contraceptives. Renewed panic jolted her and she began to count days.

Ashen-faced, she turned back to the menhir, trying hard not to believe that it was somehow aware of her presence. She was in the middle of her cycle, the most fertile period.

Her hand stole to her waist while she tried to convince herself that making love didn't lead to pregnancy each time.

Moving slowly, she walked back into the clearing, her frown heavy as she stopped by the standing stone and gazed unseeingly at it.

Gabe's child, she thought, and her whole heart yearned. Forcing herself to be practical, she considered the morning-after pill. Revulsion gripped her. No, she thought incoherently. Oh, no. And put her hand up to her eyes. Her fingers brushed the menhir. Shock lanced through her and she jerked back to stare at the ancient carved stone, wondering if she had truly felt a singing urgency, a subliminal thrumming at some deep, cellular level.

No, she'd imagined it. But she wasn't going to touch the thing again. Skin prickling, she stepped a safe distance away and thrust the prospect of pregnancy into the too-hard basket in her mind.

OK, so she was jittery. Well, she was allowed to be, surely? It wasn't every day that she woke up in a castle in the mountains, kidnapped by a man who was sure she'd stolen his priceless family heirloom, and then made unprotected love with him in a setting that produced wild fantasies!

What the hell did Gabe think he was going to do with her? Revenge? She shivered. Now that she'd seen him in the Wolf's Lair, she could imagine Gabe seeking revenge; he'd changed from the super-sophisticated man who only lost his cool when they made love. Given his coldly analytical mind and his ruthlessness, why else would he go to all the trouble of getting her here?

She turned away from the standing stone and walked across to the crumpled rug. Stooping, she picked it up.

Beneath it the grass was flattened and crushed by the force of their lovemaking.

Heart contracting into a leaden lump in her chest, she folded the rug and thrust it into the pack. A faint sound brought her head up. Eyes dilating, she watched Gabe lead the two horses between the trees. She bit on her bottom lip, then winced; their kisses had been fierce and her lip felt tender.

When the Queen's Blood hadn't turned up on the market, he'd have looked at the situation with his usual formidable detachment.

He knew exactly which weapon to use against her—her own total lack of willpower where he was concerned.

And she, idiot that she was, had fallen into his trap. Last night's kisses would have been part of his strategy; he'd tested her to see if time and distance had dulled their mutual hunger or given it a keener edge.

He must have been delighted when her helpless response had proved just how vulnerable she still was to his intense charisma.

The next step must have been obvious, she thought fiercely, eyes fixed on his ruthless, handsome face as he moved easily towards her with the horses—seduction!

Colour burned along her cheekbones, then ebbed. Humiliation ate into her, but, hell, she knew how to deal with that! And this time she was forewarned. There'd be no more trips with him, and definitely no more lovemaking. He might want her—he *did* want her—but she had to remember that he wanted his family treasure much more.

And if—if—today had given them a child, she'd go back to Fala'isi and rear it herself without telling him.

'All right?' he said, eyes narrowing as he halted the horses.

'Yes, I'm fine.' Her automatic answer drew his brows together, but he said nothing more.

They rode down the mountainside with the minimum of conversation, Gabe acting as tour guide. He did it very well—but then he'd been brought up on the legends and history of his ancestors.

Outside her bedroom door at the castle she said, 'I'll need someone to show me the rooms you want redecorated.'

His brows lifted. 'That won't be necessary,' he told her, his tone coolly dismissive.

Sara's chin jutted and she met his eyes with a frosty hauteur. 'You wanted it done; I'm going to do it. Your study and dining room are beautiful, but you can't deny that my bedroom at least needs rescuing. It's a travesty.'

He surveyed her stubborn face with amusement. 'All right. I'll get changed and come back.'

Safe for a few minutes, she showered, soaping every inch of skin as though she could wash Gabe's possession away. She tried to push the memory of their passionate encounter into a recess in her mind and lock the door on it, although it was difficult when she noticed the occasional slight contusion on her skin. She'd marked him, too, her nails digging into his back as ecstasy overtook her.

'Enough of that,' she told her reflection as she towelled herself dry. She needed to think, not dwell obsessively on the involuntary response of her body.

She donned an entirely new outfit from the skin out, noting that the clothes in the big armoire had been pressed. Clearly there was a maid here, as well as Webster.

Good, she looked businesslike and neat. When Gabe

saw her he'd know immediately that she hadn't dressed to attract—the zip-fronted shirt was loose enough to hide her breasts and her trousers were tailored. Beneath them she wore flat tassel-fronted moccasins in basic black.

Boring!

A swift rummage in her tote bag produced her notepad and measuring tape. She combed her hair back from her face and sat down at the desk, making notes on the room.

The sharp tap at the door brought her head up sharply.

An uneasy excitement slithered along her nerves; she straightened her shoulders and got up, calling, 'Just a moment,' as she gathered up pad and tape and pen.

Telling herself that to allow her body any power in this situation would be courting disaster with open arms, she walked sedately across the room and opened the door.

Instead of Gabe's dominant presence, her eyes met those of a woman she'd never expected to see again—Marya. Astonished, she opened her mouth, but no words came.

The elderly woman beamed at her, and in her thickly accented English said, 'So, you come! Is good.'

Astonished, Sara stared at her. This woman had stolen the Queen's Blood and cheerfully let her take the blame. Yet there was no malice in her dark eyes, nothing but what seemed to be transparent pleasure.

'Why is it good?' Sara managed to say inanely.

Marya smiled and took the notepad and pen and tape from her hands. 'Because you come back,' she said, and stood back to let Sara out before closing the door behind her.

'Gabe—'

'Talking, talking, talking—to Africa, I think.' Marya dismissed Gabe and Africa with a shrug. 'You want to see rooms? All right? I show you.'

What followed was bizarre. Marya chatted away as she

took her into two other bedrooms, held the end of the tape while Sara measured, and stayed respectfully silent when Sara wrote down information. It was as though the older woman didn't understand that there should be tension between them.

In fact, she did more than ignore it. She set herself out to entertain—pointing out views from various windows, telling Sara stories of people who'd lived in the castle, of long-ago events, of scenes that resonated with the authentic aura of war and history.

And she talked about Gabe, clearly idolising him. 'So good,' she said fervently. 'Is loved in the valley already. And so much man! Is master to be proud of, man to follow.'

If Marya's smiles meant anything, she didn't seem to mind that Sara had little to say in return. Did she think Sara didn't *know*?

In the end, she couldn't bear it. 'Marya, why did you take the Queen's Blood?'

She watched the maid keenly, but not a muscle moved in the lined old face. Baffled, Sara went on urgently, 'You must realise how much Gabe wants to see it again. If you love him so much, why don't you give it back to him?'

Shrugging elaborately, Marya said, 'You are here now.'

And from the door Gabe said, in a voice that chilled the blood in Sara's veins, 'That's enough. Thank you, Marya, I'll take over now.'

The maid smiled at him, gave Sara an even bigger smile, and left the room, her back straight and her spine like a steel rod.

Gabe turned to Sara. 'Leave her alone,' he said, each word filled with the cold menace of a whip-crack. 'This is between you and me; I won't have you harassing Marya.'

'What's she doing here?'

He lifted his brows in cold distaste. 'She works here,' he said icily. 'I told the butler to help you, but it seems she thought it more seemly if she did.'

Sara spared a sympathetic thought for the butler; Gabe's tone indicated that the man had felt the lash of his tongue.

A faint spasm of nausea gripped her, then ebbed. She didn't care, she told herself stonily. Trying to sound composed and practical, she said, 'It doesn't matter. I've finished what I need to do; I'll go back to my room and work on it.'

He said, 'You don't know what I want.'

Angry, because she felt a sneaking pleasure at the thought of spending time with him, she cast a disparaging glance around the room—another appalling mess of fake Louis Quinze furniture amidst a riot of gilding and scrolls and very bad Victorian art. 'Anything would be better than this,' she said with crisp emphasis.

He nodded and held open the door for her to leave. 'Almost,' he agreed. 'We'll go down to the study and discuss the way I want the place to look.'

His study, thankfully stripped of every bit of gimcrack trumpery, came as a relief. The panelled walls glowed a warm, soft gold, and the Renaissance chimneypiece that dominated the room was perfectly in keeping with a Gothic cupboard and another splendid ancestor, this one in full armour on a large, menacing horse.

'Very appropriate,' Sara said significantly, nodding at the picture.

He nodded, gesturing to her to sit down in one of the big, comfortable armchairs. 'He was Alex, the man who eventually became the first Prince of Illyria in our house. The suit of armour is still in the corridor,' he said.

'So there were princes before your ancestor took over?'

He nodded. 'Alex killed the previous one in hand-to-hand combat, then reinforced his victory by marrying the dead Prince's daughter,' he said calmly.

'What a splendid basis for a marriage!' Sara spared a compassionate thought for the long-dead princess who'd been forced to marry her father's murderer.

'By all accounts it was very happy,' Gabe said aloofly.

Uneasy, because she hated the way he seemed able to read her mind, she said stiffly, 'I suppose it was better than dying.'

He shrugged. 'She wouldn't have been killed. Her other alternative was a convent, and from what the family stories tell of her character she'd have hated that. She and Alex had eight children, and no one ever said anything about him taking a mistress.'

The words hung in the air as Webster—not Marya, Sara was glad to see—entered with a tray.

'Will you pour?' Gabe asked when they were alone again.

It was coffee. Just what she needed. She handed him a cup, black and sinful, poured milk into her own and ignored the small cakes. Keep it professional, she told herself.

'Is this the sort of atmosphere you want in the bedrooms?' she asked. 'Because if it is, finding authentic furniture of the period is not only going to be difficult, it's going to cost you a vast amount of money. Renaissance chests and coffers of museum quality, like the one in here, are practically impossible to lay hands on.'

Then she felt immediately foolish, because of course Gabe Considine, cousin to the Prince of Illyria and hugely successful magnate, wouldn't have to worry about cost.

He leaned back in his chair and said coolly, 'You can do anything you like.'

Stunned, she blurted, 'You've never seen any of my

work.' Then realised that he probably wasn't even going to look at her sketches and notes and suggestions.

'So?' His lifted brows made her feel small. 'You dress beautifully. I'm sure you have the style to dress a room as well.'

Insulted, she said, 'Not all stylish dressers can decorate a room! Tell me what you like.'

He shrugged. 'I'll be spending each summer here, so I want comfort that defers to history. This is a twelfth-century castle and that's what it should look like. Any modernising should be discreet; you've experienced the plumbing, so you know roughly what needs to be done there. I'll be interested to see what you come up with.'

Coffee drunk, he rose to his feet, apologising because he had work to do. 'Webster, make sure that Ms Milton gets safely back to her room,' he said to the butler, who'd come in to clear the coffee away.

He smiled at Sara, but his eyes reminded her that she was a prisoner.

Resentfully, Sara watched him go, then said to the butler, 'You don't have to babysit me. I'm sure I can find my own way there.'

'It's no trouble, madam,' he said colourlessly.

Once in her room she sat down and began to make notes of their conversation, getting it all down before she forgot. It was probably wasted effort.

She flung down her pen. 'I know just how the princess in the tower must have felt,' she muttered, and got to her feet. On the way back she'd glimpsed a flash of colour through a window—flowers. If the butler hadn't locked her in she'd go looking for them.

To her astonishment, she found that the door opened and the lift worked. Walking quietly, she passed suits of armour and more ancestors, posing on various horses and accompanied by several women, all looking regal and—yes, she thought, they *did* look happy.

And then she must have taken a wrong turning, because she came to a doorway that opened out onto a glorious arcaded passageway, four-square around a huge light-well open to the sky.

Sara's delighted gaze was held by pots of geraniums on the sun-warmed stone balustrades. Ancient carved marble columns held up a vaulted ceiling covered in vivid paintings of fruit and flowers, and beneath them on the interior wall someone had painted a fresco of people and animals and medieval buildings.

Enchanted, she peered at them for some minutes before her eyes found something she recognized—a careful painting of the standing stone.

'Of course,' she breathed, noticing sketchy outlines of the mountains above, and the defined notch that must be the pass.

Centuries before, someone had painted a representation of the valley and thc surrounding lands—possibly of the estates that went with the castle. Intermingled with the panorama were heraldic insignia, what appeared to be family trees, Latin sentences and scenes of village and castle life, all painted with a joyous exuberance that charmed the eye and warmed her heart.

She looked down past other doors and windows opening out onto the arcade, then walked—almost on tiptoe—to the balustrade and looked up to the next floor at another walkway, with more geraniums and several large pots of flowers softening the plain white paint there.

A soft chuckling from below drew her to lean over the balustrade and peer down into a garden divided in four by small rills of water, with a fountain in the middle. Although autumn was well on the way, flowers still bloomed in the beds—roses, and others she vaguely recognised. The scarlet leaves of the vines climbed towards the sky.

It was a delicious fantasy—lovely ease for the eye in this solid mass of stone devoted to war and power.

Built to give pleasure to a woman, Sara was sure, and envied that unknown wife who'd been loved enough to be accorded this beauty.

'It was built around the end of the sixteenth century,' Gabe said from behind her. 'The incumbent Grand Duchess was delicate, so her husband built this for her. He had the columns brought in from a Greek temple on the coast.'

Sara didn't turn. Eyes on the fountain, she said, 'He must have loved her.'

'The lords of the Wolf's Lair always marry for love.'

But a note of cynicism sharpened his bored tone, wounding her in some unknown place.

CHAPTER EIGHT

HOT with guilt, as though she'd been caught peeping through a keyhole, Sara straightened up. 'I'm sorry if I'm intruding,' she said. 'I took a wrong turning inside and found myself here, and it's so pretty....' Her voice trailed away as she met Gabe's level gaze.

'The only good thing my bastard cousin did when he took over Illyria,' he said without inflection, 'was to protect the family heirlooms. I'll take you to your room.'

He stood back to let her go ahead. She glanced through an open door as she went, and was surprised. No comfortable study, this, but a modern office set up with computers and enough electronic equipment to staff a complete business.

'This way,' Gabe said, taking Sara's elbow and steering her towards a door. 'Are you looking for something?'

The way out. But she wasn't going to tell him that. Ignoring the tiny rills of pleasure his light touch summoned, she said crisply, 'I noticed the flowers through a window and decided to see where they were.'

He appeared to accept that, but at her door he said in a coolly satirical voice, 'Give up, Sara. Even if you get out of the castle you won't get away. And if you try again I'll lock your door on you all the time.'

With a glittering, defiant look she opened the door and went inside, shutting it behind her. She waited for the click, but none came; he had to be completely confident that she wouldn't get away.

Baulked, she stared around at the horrible decor and thought of the dining room, its furniture fitting the ambience of the castle without pretension, and entirely suitable.

She started to make sketches, then remembered Gabe's savage comment about the usurper looking after the family heirlooms. After a moment's thought she pulled the bell-rope.

Five minutes later she was listening to the butler say, 'Yes, there are storerooms, but I'm sorry, I have no idea what's in them.'

'Very well, then. Thank you.' No doubt he was still smarting from the telling-off he'd got about letting Marya come up in his place.

And if anyone knew of the contents of those storerooms it would be Marya, she thought grimly.

Somehow she wasn't surprised when a knock interrupted her a few minutes later. She called out 'Come in,' and braced herself.

Marya entered, saying without preliminaries, 'You looking for old stuff?'

'Yes, I am.'

Marya nodded. 'Grand Duke say is OK. So come.'

'Grand Duke?' As they went down in the lift, Sara said, 'I thought the dictator abolished all titles in Illyria. Has the Prince restored them?'

Dark eyes half-closed, the maid shrugged. 'Always Grand Duke for us, but Prince Alex decide to—to make official?' She looked at Sara for confirmation that she'd found the right word. When Sara nodded, she said, 'Just after you engage to Grand Duke. Two—three days after.'

'Really?' A cold emptiness beneath her ribs warned Sara that she wasn't going to like the implications of the maid's offhand comment.

Marya said, 'Very big. Very—' She struggled for a moment, finally producing, 'Very important, yes?'

'Yes, I suppose it is,' Sara said quietly.

Had Gabe decided that the woman he'd asked to marry him wouldn't be a suitable wife for a Grand Duke of Illyria?

The lift stopped and the doors slid open, revealing what had probably once been dungeons. No, that had to be wrong. After all, his cousin had married a New Zealand woman whose only background had been in science! Not only that, Princess Ianthe was a little shy, and a horrific accident had given her a slight limp. Yet she was very popular with the Illyrians.

But then, that had been a love match.

Perhaps the prospect of being confirmed in the title his ancestors had borne, with its dynastic overtones, had made Gabe look more carefully at the woman he'd fallen passionately in lust with.

Perhaps he'd decided she was excellent mistress material, but unsuitable to be the mother of his children. The Prince's wife had a family whereas Sara suspected that she had been born illegitimate. Her mother would never speak of her father.

Had the suspicion that he might have made a horrendous mistake coloured his attitude to her when the Queen's Blood had disappeared?

'Here,' the maid said, unlocking a wooden door with a key so big it must have been the original.

Sara's first impression of the dark room, lit only by a couple of bare bulbs, was that it held everything that had ever been discarded in the place for the past hundred years.

Dismayed, she looked at the piles of furniture and said, 'We need to catalogue it.'

Marya gave a massive shrug. 'I know where they come from,' she said. 'I remember. Now, what you want?'

That night, another glass of champagne in her hand, her body alive with awareness, Sara asked indignantly, 'Why on earth did he replace all that lovely solid stuff, probably made by the castle carpenters or craftsmen from the valley, with ghastly second-rate Victorian copies of French rococo furniture? What was he thinking of?'

'Putting his stamp on the place,' Gabe said lethally.

She glanced at him. 'You said something about him being illegitimate,' she said tentatively.

'I called him a bastard, but not in that sense. His insistence that he wasn't legitimate was a lie.'

His tone didn't encourage questions, but she asked, 'Why?' anyway.

'It gave him a certain cachet with the ragtag adventurers and criminals and revolutionaries who initially put him in power. One aristocrat bringing down another is nowhere near as romantic as the despised bastard of the ruling house fighting to free the common people from his degenerate despot of a cousin.'

'I suppose not,' she said slowly. 'But somehow I got the idea that the deposed Prince wasn't a degenerate despot.'

He gave an odd smile and tossed back the rest of his glass of wine. 'He wasn't. And the usurper's poor bloody followers soon found out they'd been conned by an expert.'

'One with no taste,' she said, reminded that among the thousands of people the dictator had killed were Gabe's grandparents and quite a few of his other relatives. While they'd been looking through the storeroom, Marya had told her stories of their valiant fight against the man who'd driven them out of Illyria.

She said briskly, 'At least he didn't burn the furniture he discarded. If this were my castle—'

Gabe's sardonic smile stopped her.

Smarting, and angry with herself for giving him the opportunity, she doggedly continued, 'I'd strip all the panelling right back to the wood and polish it. Then I'd catalogue the furniture. From the pretty cursory look I had in the dungeons, some of it needs restoring, but most is in pretty good condition.'

He looked at her with something like a glimmer of surprise.

Defensively, she said, 'Surely you didn't think I'd suggest you go in for modern minimalism!'

'No,' he said drily. 'I suppose I'm surprised that you feel the atmosphere so strongly.'

Sara gave him a dulcet smile that should have made him very alert. 'Just because I grew up in the tropics doesn't mean I can't appreciate old things,' she purred with sweet aggression. 'I wouldn't have lasted ten minutes in my job if I didn't have some sense of the fitness of things.'

The minute she'd said it she knew she'd delivered yet another opportunity for him to be scathing, but this time he ignored the chance to remind her that for the past year her job had been on his sufferance.

Hurriedly she went on, 'Do you want every stick of furniture put back in its original place? Marya is confident that she remembers what room everything was in.'

His dark brows creased. 'You and she seem to be getting on rather well.'

Why not? Marya knew her position was totally secure. Sara kept the cynical observation to herself, however. She probably had the rest of the week here; she had to stick it out, and making comments about the woman who'd stolen the Queen's Blood would be counter-productive. The other thing she had to do was not allow herself to be seduced by Gabe again.

Instinct told her he wouldn't force her. She just had to be unobtrusive and steer away from any comments or behaviour that could be taken as provocative.

Yet, as always, Gabe's presence stimulated and challenged her. Just being with him was acutely exciting, but even more so was the heady tension that lurked beneath the ebb and flow of the conversation. It was the disturbing aftermath of their passion that morning, of heat and dangerous desire, and the memory of pleasure so exquisite it shortened her breath even now.

Her pulses quickened every time the flames flared in the fireplace, playing on his boldly chiselled features, gilding the bronze skin and autocratic cheekbones. It became an insidious torture, whittling away her defences. She'd been in the castle barely twenty-four hours, yet making love to Gabe had already wiped out the past year of anguish, with its hard-won retreat into dull acceptance.

Every sense honed, she fixed her eyes on the leaping firelight, but that only served to emphasise the effect of his voice, its subtle texture and controlled inflections tempting her. She felt alive again—her mind eager and alert, her body sleek with satisfied passion, yet yearning for more of the rapturous excitement only Gabe could give her.

The same body that even now might be pregnant.

The thought should have terrified her, but it added to the dizzy intensity of sitting in this castle, home of his forefathers, and playing her part in the thrust and parry of conversation with him.

In the end she couldn't bear it any more. She hid a faked yawn with one hand and stood up. 'Goodnight,' she said quietly.

He rose, towering over her, hooded eyes cool and cynical. 'Sleep well, Sara.'

Fat chance! she thought inelegantly, but the intonation he put into her name sent secret shudders the length of her spine. 'I will.'

At the door of her bedroom he said, 'Try not to dream too vividly.'

She faltered, but caught herself up and went into her room. 'I almost never remember my dreams,' she said lightly.

'Lucky you.'

The raw emphasis in his tone stayed with her after the door had closed on him.

Once safely inside she looked around, forcing her turbulent mind away from the physical hunger that clamoured through her. Potent as it was, it was less frightening than the deep, intense longing she recognised as love.

Yet how could she be so weak? How could she love him after his betrayal?

At least now she understood why he'd taken Marya's word over hers. She'd even been aware of the title; although he'd never used it, various gossip magazines had referred to it. But she hadn't realised that Illyria meant anything to him, because when they'd been together he'd rarely mentioned it.

In the past twenty-four hours she'd seen another dimension to the polished, astute tycoon she'd fallen in love with. Beneath the physical magnetism and dominant good looks was someone brought up to respect responsibilities, to accept the legends and magic of his countrymen.

So when he'd had to choose between the totally unsuitable woman he'd reluctantly fallen in lust with and the loyal servant who'd protected his family's treasured heirloom during the dark years, his decision had probably been inevitable.

Her mouth twisted in a grimace of pain. It should ease some of her humiliation that she now had a better idea of Gabe's motivation. The magnificent Queen's Blood meant much more to him than its monetary value—perhaps even more than its historical importance to his family. There were strong emotional links to the jewels, a semi-mystical attachment that easily overrode the reluctant sexual attraction he felt for her.

And the lords of the Wolf's Lair had been bred to be ruthless. So he'd just cut her off after that last searing interview: all she'd had from him was a brief note telling her not to contact him again, as though she'd been a servant dismissed for dishonesty.

It had shattered her.

Yet, although she understood him better, nothing had changed since she'd arrived at the Wolf's Lair, she thought, chilled and desperate. Oh, they'd made love, but it meant little beyond the fact that they couldn't keep their hands off each other.

She'd never be content with anything less than love. And perhaps Gabe had realised that he wouldn't be, either; after all, the lords of the castle had always married for love. She thought of the charming vaulted arcade, a gift to an adored wife.

Although the room was warm, she shivered and hugged herself. What had happened had happened; even though her life seemed to be careering out of control it was useless to wish she hadn't made love with him.

And if there was a baby—well, she'd deal with that when it ceased being a possibility and became a certainty.

Better to think of what she could do with this room and the two others she'd inspected that day, both clones of hers when it came to meretricious bad taste. Decorating, at least, she could manage.

She forced herself to imagine the bedroom as it should be—its pine panelling stripped clean of the white paint and restored to a warm gold. Then she'd replace the second-rate furniture with spare, appropriate pieces, and banish the elaborate crimson drapes around the bed, substituting some of the faded, elegant hangings she'd seen in the storeroom.

She sat down at the desk and began to make more notes and sketches for her mood board, until the swift tattoo of her heartbeat faded into regularity and she thought she might be able to sleep.

As she headed into the bathroom, she wondered if she'd imagined the harsh hunger underlying Gabe's final words. *Lucky you*, he'd said, as though his sleep was tormented by dreams.

Her mouth curved cynically. She must have imagined it. After all, he could have any woman he wanted, and he was utterly convinced that she'd betrayed him; *he* wouldn't be tossing in his bed because the only person he loved lacked enough trust to believe him!

Neither did he have to worry about being pregnant.

Some time during the night she woke with a start, her pulses pounding and sweat standing out on her brow. Wrenching herself upright against the pillows, she stared around, eyes wide and shocked, straining to hear the noise that had woken her—the demanding, insistent cry of a baby. *Her* baby, she knew. But the dream faded rapidly as she realised where she was.

After a few silent moments she relaxed and slid back down beneath the duvet. A confused melange of images and noises still jumbled across her brain, all faintly sinister. But although she could still feel the weight of the Queen's Blood around her throat, she couldn't remember anything else.

And then she heard the snick of the key in the lock. Eyes stretched to their widest, she watched the door open and Gabe come swiftly into the room, his powerful body outlined against the light in the stone passage outside.

'What's the matter?' he demanded, striding across to the bed.

'Nothing.' He hadn't put the light on, but she twitched the sheet up to her throat and lay rigid with apprehension. He hadn't bothered to dress, or even pull on a robe, and she'd reacted instantly and irresponsibly to the sight of his lean form, bronzed and gleaming in the dim light.

'I heard you cry out.'

'Through walls as thick as this?'

He shrugged, looking down at her with drawn brows. 'Your windows are open and so are mine,' he said, adding ironically, 'And there's not much competition. Nights here are quiet.'

'I'd noticed,' she said wearily. 'I'm sorry I woke you—I'm fine. It was just a nightmare, and now it's gone.'

The source was obvious; freed from the strictures of reason, her unconscious had transformed her concern about pregnancy into images.

'You were shouting, "The baby! Get the baby," and then you screamed,' he said neutrally.

'I—oh.'

Great response! She moistened her dry lips before starting again. 'Well, I don't remember any of it, so it can't have been too bad.' Although she tried to banish all defensiveness from her tone, she suspected she hadn't entirely succeeded.

I have to get out of here, Gabe thought, savagely aware

of unsubtle signals from his body. He still wanted her, even though she was a liar and a thief.

Had she lied about her lack of contraception?

He scanned her face, all seductive shadows and white skin against hair that tumbled across the pillows. She lay perfectly still beneath the covers, her slender body taut as a bow. He forced himself to ignore the familiar ache of desire that knotted his insides.

She hadn't been able to sell the Queen's Blood; had she decided that the prospect of a child would be one way to inveigle herself back into his life? After this morning's stupidity she'd be certain he couldn't resist the potent lure of her sexuality, and she must know he'd never turn his back on a child of his.

Not if he was sure it was his, he thought coldly, banishing an image of Sara with the little girl in the village, her arms around the child, her voice soft and soothing, as though wicked iron hooves didn't dance and fret only a few inches from her head.

And her power extended only over his body; his mind remained his own.

'Do you want anything?' he asked.

The silence stretched out, driving him towards the edge of sexual recklessness. If he slid in beside her she wouldn't refuse him. Those soft curves, that sweet fire and passion would be his. And, damn, but he wanted them—he wanted her to kiss him, to caress him with her soft, tentative touches, to open herself to him and give him those brief, glorious moments of oblivion when he could forget what she was and lose himself in her.

Sweat sprang out on his brow; every muscle in his body contracted. There was nothing civilised about his reaction to Sara; its strength mocked his self-possession and the cold, disciplined integrity he valued so highly. Only with Sara was he as possessive and territorial as a caveman.

He hated the loss of control. It took the sum total of his steely determination to rein in that humiliating hunger and fight back a surge of lust so fierce it was all he could do not to rip back the blankets and take her.

'No, I don't want anything, thank you,' she said, so low he barely heard the words.

'I'll see you in the morning, then.'

Sara turned her head into the pillow, gritting her teeth against the desire to call him back.

He'd come. Even in the darkness she'd sensed the intensity of his regard. The wild craving inside her had deepened and grown stronger, so that she'd had to clench her hands at her sides to stop herself from holding them out, welcoming him into her bed and her body and her heart.

Once the door was safely closed behind him she got up and went into the bathroom, pouring herself a glass of water. She drank it down greedily, then turned on the shower, shuddering as the cold water hit her heated, super-sensitive skin.

A rough towelling banished all signs of arousal except for her slowly smouldering inner core. No more sleep tonight, she thought, and slipped into a robe before walking across to the nearest window. She leaned out and breathed in the cool, fresh air. Beneath the walls the valley spread out in a patchwork of silver and black, bewitched into glamour by the magic of the moon, and so beautiful it intensified her pagan, unslaked craving for the man who lay in his dark room a few feet away through the thick stone walls.

Far to the north, moonlight glinted on snow, and her heart twisted and tears stung her throat and eyes.

She drew back from the windows with their six-sided

panes of glass, each one delivering a slightly different view of the valley, and went across to the desk. Switching on the lamp, she sat down and began to read her notes.

The loud *whump-whump-whump* of a helicopter's rotors woke her from sleep. She lay stupidly in the bed, trying to remember where she was and what she was doing.

Last night, she thought dimly, remembering the hours spent at her desk before she'd crawled back into bed by the light of a setting moon. She'd dropped off to sleep as though she'd been hit on the head.

Her eyes flew open, only to blink against the bright day outside. She leapt out of bed to run across the room and crane out of the window. The helicopter had landed on the other side of the castle; she turned back into the room, snatching up her robe when a knock sounded on the door.

The door opened before she'd shrugged into it. Flushing, she glanced at Gabe's stony face, then hauled the lapels over her scanty chemise and briefs.

With no sign of emotion, Gabe said, 'I'm sorry, but I've been called away. I should be back in a few days.'

She stared at him. 'I see.'

'Do you?' His smile was tight and humourless. 'I suspect you do.'

And he crossed the room in a couple of long strides, pulled her into his arms and kissed her, as though he were one of his forefathers setting out to war. Perhaps he was; Sara knew enough to understand that although his life wasn't in danger, every time he made a decision he risked the well-being and the future of not only himself but thousands of people who depended on his icy intelligence and his honesty to keep their jobs safe. And that didn't include the millions of people who trusted him with their money.

The responsibility was just as great as it had been for those forebears of his who'd ridden out of the Wolf's Lair into battle to protect their people and their country.

So she kissed him back with passionate fervour, lifting herself on tiptoe to run her fingers through his hair, giving him her mouth freely while he stamped his bold possession on her lips and her heart.

Too soon he lifted his head and released her, his narrowed eyes molten in the hard, arrogant planes of his face.

'Don't have any more nightmares,' he said roughly, that uncompromising air of power and authority very pronounced.

Her smile was touched with sadness. 'Not even you can forbid them.'

Some reckless emotion glinted like blue fire in his eyes. 'Want to bet?' he drawled. 'Remind me of that when I come back.'

Eyes enormous in her white face, Sara watched him go, then stood at her window to watch the chopper rise from behind the castle and lift into the sky before turning to head over the mountains. She followed it with her eyes until it was a mere point in the brilliant blue sky, then blinked several times as the bright morning sky brought moisture to her eyes.

Clearly something had gone wrong somewhere in his vast business empire.

Emptily she dressed and drifted across to the desk, looking at the work she'd done the previous night.

It was rough, but good—some of the best she'd done. So it was truly ironic that Gabe wasn't going to accept anything from her. Nevertheless, he'd commissioned a plan, so that was what he'd get.

A knock on the door heralded a breakfast tray. Sara thanked the young maid who brought it in and set it on the bedside table. Alone again, she felt her stomach clench. How on earth was she going to get rid of a rack of toast, a bowl of fruit and another of creamy yoghurt? She didn't want to upset whoever had gone to such trouble.

Amongst the delicious food stood a small silver vase with a rosebud, softly crimson, in it. Her eyes filled with tears. It was a charming thought, but if only Gabe had picked it for her…

CHAPTER NINE

FROM the depths of an armchair, Sara looked up from the rough plans she was checking and smiled. Across the bedroom the young maid wielded a cloth and a large pot of honey-scented beeswax, humming as she polished a chest that had just arrived up from one of the storerooms, courtesy of two strong men. Once the walls were stripped back to their original state, the simple wooden piece would settle into the room as if it had been made for it—as, perhaps, it had.

'Thank you,' Sara said in Illyrian—one of the phrases she'd learned during the past four days.

The maid gave a shy smile, but it was clear she wanted Sara out of the bedroom while she went about her usual chores. Picking up her notepad and pen, Sara left her to it and headed for the vaulted arcade.

But once there she dropped pad and pen onto a wooden settle and leaned on the balustrade, soaking in the glory of a day as crisp and golden as an apple in the sun.

Gabe hadn't contacted her. Not that she'd expected him to, so why did it hurt? Perhaps he'd realised how outrageous he'd been in kidnapping her and planned to stay away until she left.

It would be for the best, she told herself sturdily, fighting the deep-seated ache inside her with a flash of bitterness.

Four days ago she'd arrived here filled with hope that this would be the career advance she so fiercely wanted. Her mouth tightened and she stared unseeingly at a great pot of scarlet geraniums. She should be delighted at the prospect of not seeing Gabe again.

However, he clearly didn't intend her to leave without permission; the first night he'd been away she'd tried her door, only to find it locked. Transient colour stung her cheeks; no doubt the butler wondered why it was his job to lock his master's lover in at night.

No, she thought, lifting her face to the sun, it wouldn't be Webster. Gabe would have chosen Marya to be her gaoler.

A decision that had been slowly forming in her mind crystallised. Pregnant or not, she'd go back to Fala'isi. In the outside world Gabe's power extended too far, but on the island she'd be safe. The Chapman family who lived there were her friends, and they had the power to keep anyone off Fala'isi. Even world-famous billionaires, she thought with painful irony.

But before she left Illyria she'd make another appeal to Marya to give Gabe back the rubies. And then she'd leave everything behind her, forge a new life in the island tourist industry, and eventually forget about Gabe.

Another lie. Her throat tightened. He was engraved on her heart, on her mind, so much a part of her that the cruellest betrayal and a year apart hadn't been enough to protect her from more heartache. She'd remember everything, from the flowers she'd picked yesterday to the innermost depths of the storerooms she'd plundered.

And Gabe….

In uncanny echoing of her thoughts, he said from

behind her, 'I hear you've been turning the place upside down.'

Stunned, yet somehow not surprised, she turned slowly. He was standing in the doorway of his office, tall and dominating and utterly beloved. His enigmatic face was shadowed by the vaulted ceiling, whereas the sun beat down on her head and shoulders, revealing every expression. He looked tired, she thought with a clutch of apprehension, as though the business trip had exhausted his splendid vitality.

'I wanted to show you how the castle could be returned to honesty,' she said, hearing the lilt in her voice with a shocked surprise.

His brows rose. 'Honesty?' A subtle taunt infused his voice.

Sara could have kicked herself for using that particular word, but she insisted stoutly, 'The way it is now—apart from the dining room, parlour and study—is horribly, glaringly *dis*honest. As well as being a murderer and a tyrant, your cousin had no taste and no understanding. This is a castle, not a château, and the furniture and decor should reflect that.'

She stopped, feeling exposed.

'Go on,' he said noncommittally, a frown drawing his black brows together.

'So to give you an idea of what should be done I've moved the junk out of my room and put in pieces I found in the storerooms,' she said curtly. 'By the way, a man—one of the outlying farmers, I think—arrived yesterday with a magnificent French armoire. He said it belonged to you, and he'd heard through the grapevine that you wanted all the furniture back. How did he get it? Marya didn't explain.'

'The dictator ordered everything destroyed,' Gabe said.

Horrified, she stared at him. 'Why?'

His broad shoulders lifted a negligent moment. 'Destruction was all he understood,' he said calmly.

'What changed his mind?'

'The villagers waited until he'd left, then stripped the castle and smuggled the furniture out to hiding places in the valley. Some of the bigger stuff was hidden in the castle in secret rooms.'

Sara's eyes widened. 'Oh, come on now—secret rooms?'

'All castles have secret chambers,' he told her.

She said quietly, 'The villagers must have loved and respected your grandparents very much.'

'They have a tradition of loyalty. And one of looking to the castle for protection, of course.'

'Rescuing the furniture sounds much more personal than a tradition,' she said.

'Tradition can be very personal, but, yes, I'm inclined to agree with you. My grandparents were loved and respected. I'd like to have known them.' He moved from the door in the shadows and surveyed her face, his eyes coolly speculative. 'How have you enjoyed your daily rides?'

'Very much, thank you.' She added on a snap, 'Your grooms managed to keep their surveillance reasonably inconspicuous.'

Gabe hadn't bothered to contact her, but he'd certainly kept tabs on what she'd been doing! For some reason the knowledge mingled bitterness and an odd feeling of being protected.

A flash of white teeth in his dark face made her go weak at the knees. 'I told them not to be intrusive,' he said blandly. 'Show me your room.'

'Of course.'

He might hate it, and once she'd gone he wouldn't want to be reminded of her presence in any way, but decorating the room had been a labour of love.

She glanced at his impassive face as he surveyed the changes she'd made. 'I wanted to make it comfortable and welcoming without losing its aura of history and strength and its sophistication, because although it seems plain this furniture was made of the best timber by true craftsmen. It's perfectly suited to its function and the setting.'

His gaze travelled from the honey-scented chest to the bed with its subtly faded drapes, and the carpet—an antique Persian, its rich luxury echoing the colours of the drapes. Oddly enough, his survey stopped at the pot of flowers on the sill.

'Webster told me I could take flowers from the picking garden,' she said swiftly.

'Of course. You have excellent taste—as I'm sure you know.'

'I chose pictures that I thought suited the room,' she said. 'You may well have photographs of the different rooms showing where they should go—'

'That was one thing my cousin made sure of,' he interpolated in a lethally flat voice. 'He burned everything that was personal to my grandparents, but kept the armour and archives because he could claim ancestry with them.'

'I'm so sorry. I know what it's like to have nothing.'

He gave her a keen glance. 'It's only my grandparents' lives I'm missing records of. I have enough photographs of my childhood to sink a small liner. How did you lose yours?'

'Our house collapsed in a cyclone. Nothing was saved.'

'Is that when your parents died?'

'My mother.' She turned her head away, presenting him with her profile. 'I never knew my father.'

He'd forgotten that. Gabe's eyes narrowed as he studied her straight nose, the luscious curves of her mouth, the arrogant chin jutting high, and the way the sun coaxed fiery little flames in the depths of her hair. A cold, still pride radiated from her, and he felt his grip on reality suddenly shift, as though an inner eye had opened and the truth he'd been so confident of was revealed for a sham.

It only took a second or two to regain his control, to see her again as the schemer and sexual predator she was, but her power to enslave his senses made him icily furious.

Into a silence suddenly too electric, he said, 'How did you survive?'

'She tied me to a coconut palm. Mine survived the winds and the rising sea; hers was washed away.'

Was that childhood trauma the reason she'd stolen the Queen's Blood? A desperate grab for the security she'd had so cruelly stolen from her? Perhaps a security she'd never had as she hadn't known her father?

Psychobabble, Gabe told himself scornfully. And why are you looking for excuses?

Do you want her back?

His body responded to the contemptuous question with unmistakable energy. Yes, he wanted her, in every way possible—except as his wife.

She still hadn't admitted to stealing the necklace—and the fact that he was wondering whether he'd made a monumental mistake was only because he couldn't stop himself from wanting her.

Lust, he reminded himself ruthlessly, didn't care about morals. 'How old were you?' he asked.

'Fourteen.'

'And what happened then?'

She shrugged. 'My grandparents—my mother's parents—took me in. I had to leave Fala'isi to live in England.'

Not a happy outcome for her, Gabe surmised shrewdly, noting the shadows in her green-grey eyes.

He repressed another unwelcome and weakening impulse to sympathy, and asked abruptly, 'When will you know whether you're pregnant or not?'

Sara looked away, colour rising unexpectedly through her glorious skin. 'In a fortnight, give or take a few days,' she said reluctantly.

'Then it's just as well that I brought back a testing kit,' he said, each word cold and clinical, as though he were discussing the world financial market. 'Apparently it's accurate within a few days of possible conception. I'll bring it along.'

Her head whipped around. Directing a narrow, suspicious stare at him she said, 'All right.'

'And if you are pregnant we're getting married. No child of mine is going to be born a bastard.'

'Why?' she asked, adding bluntly, 'I won't ask for financial support, if that's what's worrying you.'

His expression darkened. 'It's not.'

Something in his tone alerted her. Picking her way carefully, she said, 'Is this about your cousin the dictator, who lied about being a bastard?'

'No,' he returned curtly. 'It's about accepting responsibility.'

A feverish mix of despair and panic robbed her of coherent thought. She looked into Gabe's implacable face and said hoarsely, 'Don't be silly. You can't marry me—you despise me. You think I'm a thief.'

The ugly word echoed in the bedroom.

Gabe shrugged. 'No doubt if we do marry you'll suddenly remember where you stashed the Queen's Blood.'

His mouth twisted into a sardonic smile that came too close to derision. 'I'll enjoy seducing it from you.'

'Pregnant or not, I won't be your legalised whore.' Indignation choked her; she had to stop herself from hitting him. Of all the insults! This was beyond anything he'd done before, and loving him wasn't enough to make her forgive him.

Passionately she ploughed on. 'How do you plan to deal with my supposed tendencies? By locking me up? Or supplying me with a keeper wherever I go in case I feel overwhelmed by a desire to make off with someone else's jewellery?' Pride rang in her voice, scornful and defiant. 'No, thank you—I won't spend the rest of my life being despised and watched and mistrusted. You can't force me to marry you.'

'If you're pregnant you'll do as I say,' he said, his indifferent tone harrowing nerves already stretched to breaking point. 'Even if it's just a quick marriage to legitimise the child and then an even quicker divorce.'

She breathed deeply, fire kindling green flames in her eyes. 'Do you really think I'll tamely let you take over my life? Who the hell do you think you are?' she queried savagely, barely able to spit the words out.

He gave another grin, mirthless this time. 'I'm Gabriel Considine, Grand Duke of Illyria and the Northern Marches—or so my cousin tells me,' he said, cold irony buttressing each word. 'More to the point, if you're pregnant, I'm the father of your child. And that child will know its place in the world.'

'If it's a son it might well be the next Grand Duke,' she hurled back. 'Have you thought of that? The child of a thief—'

He cut in ruthlessly. 'Son or daughter, it will have every

right to the name Considine and a position on the family tree. This is not negotiable, Sara.'

Sara gulped in a ragged breath and closed her eyes, struggling to control the mixture of feelings that rioted through her—anguish because he didn't love her, fury at his high-handedness, and a kind of fierce relief that he intended to accept responsibility for his child. But then, Gabe was big on responsibility.

'Is that all you think of?' she demanded. 'Your damned family? If there is a child I can look after it and take care of it. We won't need you. Better a father who's not there than one who's willfully blind and prejudiced and—'

'Better a *mother* who's not there than one who sleeps her way into a man's confidence and then betrays it,' he snarled.

The unspoken threat scored her like a whip, cutting into her fragile restraint and shattering it. Take her child from her? *Never!* Propelled by fear and despair, she struck him right across his beautiful mouth.

Silence tightened around them. Horrified, she stared at the darkening mark her hand had made on his skin, then into eyes of molten steel.

'Oh, God,' she whispered sickly into the strained silence. 'Gabe, I'm sorry—so sorry….'

She touched his lips, her fingers trembling in a featherlight caress. He made a muffled sound, and too late she saw the moment rage was transformed into something else.

When he reached for her she didn't resist; she lifted her face in mute invitation and said again, 'I'm so sorry.'

'It's all right,' he said, and his mouth took hers and she surrendered, as she would always, she realised with a jolt to her heart, because she loved him so much.

He kissed the soul from her body, and then lifted her and came down with her onto the bed, his ravenous mouth finding with unerring accuracy the exact place where her neck joined her shoulder.

Ecstasy shot through her like arrows; she shuddered, and tore at his shirt, her hands clumsy but determined. Laughing deep in his throat, he bit with exquisite restraint before lying back and giving her free access to him.

All finesse abandoned, she yanked his buttons free and spread out his shirt, staring with intense, acute pleasure at the smooth bronze skin, sleek and supple and hot, over the framework of long, coiled muscles.

'You smell divine,' she said huskily against his chest, her lashes making little butterfly movements on his shoulder.

'Soap,' he said thickly, one hand pulling her closer so that she could feel his urgent response, the tense hunger that had hardened every muscle in his powerful body.

'No, it's more complex than that.' Sometimes she'd woken in her lonely bed with that scent in her nostrils and she'd cried until dawn, aching with the misery of having lost him.

Her voice deepened into a sexy hoarseness. 'It's you, just you.'

His laughter lifted his chest against her, reverberated through her and set her body leaping with pleasure. 'I didn't know I had my own personal aroma.'

'Mmm. And your own personal taste, too—musky, a little salty. Delicious.' She lowered her face and licked, letting her lips and tongue glide delicately across his skin.

When he shuddered an outrageous delight filled her; no matter what happened, how they fought, what he thought of her, this was honest and true. Lust, yes, but he could no more deny it than she could.

With her forefinger she traced the whorl of silken hair across the broad, powerful expanse of his torso, finally ending at the sharp little nubbin of his nipple. Her mouth closed around it and she explored him with a wondering curiosity and an odd, deep-rooted sensation of coming home.

She expected no gentle lovemaking, no sweet delight in slow seduction, but she gasped when Gabe used his immense strength to turn her onto her back. In one rapid, confident movement he pulled the T-shirt over her head, his dark face intent and dangerously absorbed, a stain of colour across those magnificent cheekbones.

Skilfully he dispensed with her bra, tossing it away so that she lay stretched before his possessive gaze like a captive bride, her slender body flushed and acutely sensitised to his touch and the roaming inventory of his eyes, baulked only by the narrow strip of lace across her hips.

'So do you,' he said, kissing the gentle swell of her upper breast.

Drugged by desire, she murmured, 'What?'

'You have your own scent—soft and fresh and lingering.' He moved, adjusting himself and her so that he could reach the pleading centre of her breast. Deeply he said, 'And you taste like honey and cream and strawberries and champagne. Addictive as hell and impossible to forget.'

His mouth closed around the peaked nipple and she gasped again and arched into him, transfixed by heat and fire and sizzling desperation. Without volition her hands tightened on his shoulders, her body eager and molten beneath him as he coaxed her into violent arousal.

Her pulse drummed in her ears and she ached for the magic moment of union. But he refused to give her the swift, hard ferocity she longed for. Instead, he toyed with her, using his hands and his mouth and his voice, his vast experience of women and lovemaking, to send her spinning dizzily into a world of rapturous frustration.

Eventually, when her body was straining desperately against him, her whole being lost to the hunger he summoned from some hidden place deep inside her, she croaked, 'Gabe, for pity's sake—please…'

Only then did he move over her, but even then he didn't finally consummate their desire. She looked up into a face drawn with blazing sexual drive, into eyes narrowed and glittering, and her body arced into a bow against him, seeking the release only he could give her.

But he didn't take that final step into joining them.

Was he doing this deliberately? Was this his revenge—to take her to the edge and deny her the ultimate fulfilment? Sick at heart, she closed her eyes and tried to blank everything out.

'Look at me,' he commanded, his voice low and rasping.

Pride drove her lashes up.

'Sara,' he said, and drove into her, all his splendid power and compelling magnetism focused only on one thing—his complete conquest.

And she couldn't deny him, couldn't deny the reckless anticipation he'd aroused so skilfully, overpowering caution, seducing her along the path to defeat and humiliation again.

His hands beneath her hips lifted her, held her clamped against him, and he began to move inside her, the tendons in his neck tightening as he fought for control.

'No,' she said harshly, and unleashed her feminine power, winding her legs around his hips and milking him with secret inner muscles.

Anticipation grew and grew, sending out the first ripples of extreme pleasure, and then waves—waves that caught her and tossed her upwards and onwards into a rarefied stratosphere where all that mattered was the man who'd claimed her entire being and the erotic submission he wrung from her.

And then her body convulsed—lost in ecstasy, lost in Gabe—and almost immediately he followed her into that place that was theirs only, spending himself in her without thought or care or hindrance.

CHAPTER TEN

SARA lay locked in Gabe's arms, his strength wrapping her in a blanket of complete security. How could everything feel so right—when it was all so wrong?

She struggled to stay in the dazed, sensuous lassitude that had kept her silent since that final cataclysmic release. She didn't want to think, didn't want to break this magical spell, but thoughts buzzed like menacing flies through her brain.

At least he'd used protection this time. And the fact that he'd had that necessary little packet on his person—did that mean he'd decided to use *her* whenever he felt like it?

Not even the heat of his big body around her could warm the humiliation that chilled her. For a year she'd fooled herself that she could forget him, that their affair and engagement and bitter parting had been a melodramatic, wholly incongruous episode in her serene, ordinary life.

Now she had to accept that she was linked to him by something much more dangerous than passion. For some reason he was her man—the only man for her. No one else would do, she thought despairingly.

She blocked the thought, concentrating on the feel of his skin, dry now, and the sleekly powerful body that lay half beneath her. Strange that, in spite of everything that pushed them apart, only in his arms did she feel this intense security.

'What's the matter?' he asked, his voice rumbling from his chest.

Startled, she blinked. How did he know? She hadn't stirred or moved, hadn't altered her breathing, yet somehow he'd sensed the change in her.

That awareness was another thing that made him such a good businessman. He'd once told her that he never trusted anyone except on instinct; he'd laughed and called it a primitive response that warned him when someone wanted to take advantage of him.

Well, he probably no longer relied so heavily on that, she thought wearily. He was sure it had let him down badly when it came to her.

'Sara?'

'Nothing.' The word came out huskily, like a caress, and she cleared her throat and lied more strongly, 'Nothing at all.' Sometimes the truth was just too dangerous.

He slid one hand up her throat, tilting her head so that he could see her face. Panic-stricken by his probing gaze, she clamped her eyes shut. But that was too much of a giveaway; she forced them open and fixed him with a defiant stare.

She didn't like the speculative smile on his lips, but his voice was amused. 'I like that tigerish glower, but the way your eyelids droop when I'm kissing you is much more intriguing.'

Sensing his intention, Sara tried to clamp her lips together, only to feel them soften and cling when his mouth covered hers. If she didn't know better, she'd almost be able to believe that the kiss was tender, she thought dreamily, floating on the beguiling tide of afterglow and arousal, eager to lose herself in the sensuous enchantment of his touch rather than ask herself unanswerable questions.

He slid his hands around her waist and lifted her so that he could taste her breasts with exquisitely tormenting skill. Sara's breath came faster, and she shivered at the sensuous rush of hunger through her body.

She linked her arms around his neck and swayed towards him, her body curving into his.

Quietly, holding his gaze with hers, she asked, 'Why won't you believe that I had nothing to do with the disappearance of the Queen's Blood?'

Afterwards she cursed the impulse that had brought the words to her lips before she had time to censor them. But she couldn't make love with him again knowing what he thought of her. In the heat of anger, yes; never in this slow, smouldering gentleness, this simulation of love.

His big body clenched, and in a single strong movement he pushed her away and got off the bed, striding towards the window in naked splendour. Bitterness overwhelming her, Sara watched him go, each step taking him away from the only common ground they owned.

While she'd slept in his arms the late-afternoon sun had tinted the clouds over the mountains pink and copper. The reflected light caressed the lines and contours of his body, warming bronze skin and highlighting the sinuous flow and flexion of the muscles beneath. He looked, she thought with a catch to her heartbeat, like some magnificent artefact from the old Mediterranean, a careless god come down to cause turmoil and pain to a dazzled, love-struck woman.

He said harshly, 'Does it make more sense to believe that the woman who kept the secret all those years, even when her family was targeted by the tyrant—?'

'What do you mean?' she interrupted.

He struck the windowsill with a clenched fist. The overt violence shocked her; she'd always sensed his capacity for it, but his icy self-discipline had kept it leashed. Even when he'd accused her of stealing the rubies and sent her out of his life he hadn't raised his voice.

She shivered, her skin tightening at the memories. He hadn't needed to. His cutting words had flayed her to the bone.

In a cool, unemotional tone, Gabe said, 'He knew that her whole family was loyal, and that Marya had worked as maid to my grandmother. He didn't have a high opinion of women, so it never occurred to him that she'd have been entrusted with the secret. But after her father and husband died in the bastard's torture chambers, so did two of her cousins who'd also worked at the castle.'

Sara gave a horrified gasp.

'That's what it was like here.' Gabe spoke with quiet, lethal intensity. 'My grandparents were lucky—their deaths in ambush were easy compared to those who fell into my cousin's hands. Marya survived by pretending to be slightly unhinged, but she suffered torture and beatings and bitter grief to protect the Queen's Blood, and she never lost faith that we'd come back. I cannot believe she would steal the necklace.'

Sickened, Sara huddled into the puffy duvet, pulling it around her to hide her nakedness. Absently, she rubbed a slight red mark on her arm.

Gabe swore under his breath and came back to the bed.

Sara watched him warily while he held the palm of his hand over the place she'd touched.

'Did I do that?' he demanded harshly.

'I don't know,' she said on a subdued inflection, adding, 'It could be an insect bite.'

Gabe straightened and surveyed her with a burnished, opaque gaze. 'I hope so. I'm not rough with my women.'

His words brought her chin up sharply. 'I'm not one of your women,' she returned, hoping her voice was steady enough to hide the pain that clawed at her.

A cynical, humourless movement of his beautiful mouth sent another despairing quiver through her.

'Don't lie,' he said. 'One touch and you'd give me what I want.'

'Reluctantly,' she snapped.

'Yes, but that's the point.' He pulled on his trousers, his big body moving with lithe, careless grace. 'Of course it's reluctant—do you think I wanted to make love to you?'

She turned her head away and listened to his movements, matching his cold, dismissive tone when she said, 'I think that whatever this—this wretched thing is that links us, it's totally devoid of love or compassion or understanding.'

'I have to agree. A woman who would steal something and try to frame an uneducated peasant for the theft comes pretty low in my estimation. As well as being stupid. That was the first safe Marya had ever seen; she didn't understand how it worked. And you chose the number.'

'How do you know she hadn't seen a safe before?' she demanded, some dim memory niggling at her brain.

'Because she told me, and I believed her,' he said levelly.

'But she suggested the number to set.' It was obvious he didn't believe her, and she insisted. 'It was the date of your birthday.'

He gave a snort of derision.

The defeatism she felt whenever she tried to convince him boiled over into fury. Ignoring her nakedness, she sprang off the bed and stalked across to him, all wild mahogany hair and vehemently glittering eyes green as grass in her flushed face.

'The seventh of November,' she hissed, poking him in the chest with an aggressive forefinger. 'I don't care now what you think, or why you believe I did it, but *I did not take the damned necklace*.'

A whisper of cool, meadow-scented air through the window licked across Sara's skin. Shivering, she realised that she was standing naked in front of him, that he was only half dressed, and for once—the only time ever, she thought bleakly—they weren't falling onto the bed, overpowered by the need to slake this mutual lust.

For some odd reason it seemed like progress—except that one glance at Gabe's ice-blue eyes and flinty face scotched that idea.

Resisting the urge to weep, she turned away and said woodenly, 'It doesn't matter any more. Let me go, Gabe—we're just tearing each other apart, going over and over the same thing, getting nowhere.'

'Why the hell are you so stubborn?' Gabe's anger roughened his voice, but he stunned her by saying fiercely, 'If you'd just tell me why, I think I might find it in my heart to understand—to forgive.'

'Forgive?' Bitterness wrenched a short, mirthless laugh from her; it felt like shattering glass in her chest. 'If anyone needs to forgive, I should be forgiving myself, for being so stupid as to fall in love with a stubborn, stupid, inflexible, unbearable man like you. At least you made sure I soon fell *out* of love!'

She stopped, staring at him as the wisp of memory that had teased her brain suddenly solidified. 'And Marya *does* know how a safe works! Two days ago she took me into your office, unlocked the big document safe, and brought out the plans of the castle.'

Gabe's expression darkened, but after a moment he shrugged, dismissing her statement. 'She's been working in the castle all year. No doubt she's seen me use it.'

Aware now that nothing would convince him, Sara gave up. Baldly, her facial muscles stiff and tired, she said, 'I don't know what you hoped to achieve from this ridiculous kidnapping, but it's not going anywhere. I want to go. Now.'

'You'll go at the end of the week,' he said relentlessly. 'And why was Marya helping you?'

'Perhaps because she feels a little sorry for me?' she stated tautly. 'Why don't you ask her?'

She glowered at his back as he walked towards the door, the freezing chill engendered by his total lack of trust in her not dissipating when she saw the red scratches on his back, put there by her fingernails in a wild excess of passion.

Frustration and anger loosened her control over her voice. More loudly than she intended, she said after him, 'And while you're doing that why don't you ask her what she hoped to achieve by stealing the Queen's Blood?'

It was a cheap shot and he ignored it. She waited until the door closed behind him before collapsing onto the side of the bed and biting her lips to hold back the aching, humiliating tears.

She couldn't bear to stay here as a convenient mistress, used whenever he wanted her, ignored when he didn't, to be banished like a discarded dishrag once she'd convinced him she wasn't pregnant. It would destroy something vital in her—the last shred of pride.

She had to get away.

She had dressed again, in a pair of jeans and a soft jersey the exact red-brown of her hair, when she heard the clatter of a helicopter. A nameless emotion cut off her breath. Gabe was going.

Or perhaps, she thought, steadying her hand and putting down the comb, he was sending her away. Perhaps their soulless, mechanical coupling had sickened him into realising that she had to go. Pain sliced through her so sharply she gasped, but she stiffened her shoulders and spine and held her head high.

No, he wouldn't send her away until he was sure she wasn't pregnant.

But even if she were she wouldn't marry him and compound the mockery that was their relationship. No child should have to grow up knowing its father despised its mother.

A knock on her door brought her head around. Slowly, apprehensively, she said, 'Come in.'

Marya appeared, smiling as always, no sign in her cheerful wrinkled face of the torture and pain she'd endured for the sake of the Queen's Blood and the Considines. Her black eyes checked out the bed and Sara cringed. Why hadn't she pulled the covers straight? There could be no doubt what had happened there!

She searched the older woman's face for chagrin, but Marya positively beamed at her.

'His Grace say come down now,' she announced, the words ringing with pride. She surveyed Sara and nodded in satisfaction. 'Please.'

Sara stared at her. 'I—no.'

Clearly taken aback, the maid frowned. 'You must. Clothes are fine—you look good.'

'I don't want to see him.'

Marya gave a huge, exasperated sigh. 'Then the Grand Duke come up and bring you down.'

Anger spiked through Sara. She opened her mouth, but closed it again firmly. She wasn't going to throw a tantrum in front of the woman who'd deliberately wrecked her life.

'Very well, then,' she said tonelessly. 'I need to put some make-up on.'

She turned and went into the bathroom to don the only armour she possessed. Foundation first—her sheer matt one didn't provide enough camouflage, but it would be better than nothing. Eyeliner and shadow highlighted her eyes, then carefully she outlined her tender mouth with a soft raspberry lipstick. She was still too pale, so she applied a little blusher to her cheeks and stared at her reflection. Defiance sparked green in her eyes; she fished in her make-up kit and drew out a luscious fuchsia lipgloss.

'And you can make what you like of that,' she murmured when she'd applied it. At least it and the blusher stopped her from looking defeated and miserable!

She strode into the bedroom, but stopped precipitately in the doorway; Marya hadn't left and was still bustling around. She'd remade the bed and was neatly folding the shirt Gabe had left behind.

She looked up when Sara entered and grinned, bright black eyes snapping with laughter. 'Good,' she said. 'Very good.'

Sara blinked, abruptly abandoning her conviction that the maid had stolen the necklace. She couldn't be so—so blasted normal, she thought as she walked beside the older woman to the lift, if she'd taken the Queen's Blood. Right from the start Marya had seemed happy to see her, even conspiratorial, as though they were accomplices.

But if it hadn't been Marya, then who?

None of it made sense, she thought despairingly.

Marya opened the door into Gabe's study. Two men looked up, and Sara's breath caught painfully in her chest.

Individually, Gabe and his cousin were two extremely handsome men; together they were overwhelming. It was easy to see they were related; both were tall and lean and graceful, blazing with an inbuilt air of authority. Both had dark hair and bronze skin, and they shared the trademark Considine blue eyes—passed on from some Saxon princess in their heritage, Gabe had told her.

Gabe said neutrally, 'Alex, you've met Sara, of course.'

Sara smiled at the man beside him. 'It's good to see you, sir.'

Prince Alex's eyes were far too perceptive, but he smiled and shook her hand and made some inconsequential remark. In response she asked after his wife, a noted marine biologist, and his children.

Autocratic features softening, he told her of the latest escapade of the Crown Prince, an imp of eighteen months, who had inherited the Princess Ianthe's love of water.

'Swimming with dolphins is all very well,' he finished wryly, 'and of course the people insist that it's a sign that all will be well in Illyria for the next generation, but none of us know how he learned to swim. The girls—' referring to his young daughters '—insist that the dolphins taught him, and as their nurse probably told them this I assume that the people believe it, too.'

The rare dolphins of Illyria's large central lake were the prized icons of its people, figuring largely in folklore and pageantry.

What followed could have been any meeting of friends; both men had superb manners and made things easy for her, and although occasionally her composure lurched, she thought she got through the first part of the evening well. Neither man mentioned why the Prince had decided to call in at the Wolf's Lair; instead, the conversation ranged far and wide.

The frisson of awareness was always there, of course; Sara was acutely conscious of Gabe's gaze.

And the Prince knew. He must have sensed the tension the moment she walked into the room.

Later she couldn't remember what they ate for dinner; it was even difficult to recall their conversation. She could, however, picture the darkly intent look on Gabe's face as he challenged his cousin on some issue of state—and the note of enthusiasm as the two men discussed the next step in their subtle manipulation of Illyria into the ranks of modern nations.

And the way his eyes crinkled at the corners when he laughed, and the quirk of his mouth when his cousin said something that amused him—and his avoidance of any contact with her at all.

Interested in spite of herself, Sara kept her eyes guarded and fought for a clear mind, refusing to think of what had happened that afternoon. Time enough when she was sleepless in bed to let her mind dwell on each—

Stop that right now!

Eventually she rose and said, 'I'm sure you have much to talk about, so I'll leave you now.'

Both men got to their feet. 'Goodnight,' the prince said, his mouth faintly ironic. 'I'm afraid I'm going early tomorrow morning, so this will be goodbye—until I see you again.'

What did he mean by that? 'Please give my regards to your wife,' she said formally, 'and a hug for each of the girls and your son.'

'Of course.'

Once outside the room she breathed more easily, but the headache that had begun to knock during the last half-hour didn't ease. In her room she shook a painkiller into the palm of her hand, then looked down at it. If she were pregnant, it might not be a good idea. She'd refused wine both before and during dinner; Gabe's eyes had rested on her face, then moved on as he'd poured a delicious fruit concoction for her, but he knew why.

And the Prince probably suspected, she thought worriedly. Nothing much escaped him.

Why hadn't she asked him for help to get out of the castle? He was possibly the only man on earth who might be able to make Gabe let her go; it hadn't taken her long to sense the true, deep respect and affection they had for each other.

Because it would have put the Prince in an awkward position, she told herself, then grimaced. He'd coped with awkwardness before; hell, the man had walked into a country on the verge of civil war and by sheer force of personality brought about peace.

And she hadn't kept quiet because she didn't want to ruin the relationship between the two men.

No. Admit it. She wanted these final few days with Gabe.

A half-gulp, half-sob shook her. She washed the pill down the handbasin, cleaned her face and teeth and only then realised that someone had left a package in the bathroom beside her sponge bag.

Frowning, she surveyed it, her mouth shaping a soundless *Oh!* when she realised what it had to be—the pregnancy test kit.

It only took a few minutes. She stared at the little marker, and when it didn't change colour she ordered herself to be happy, to feel great, because she wasn't pregnant with Gabe's child.

But an enormous grief weighed her down with a heaviness she hadn't experienced before, not even when Gabe had so summarily dismissed her from his life. Moving slowly and carefully, she got into her nightclothes.

Her bed had been pulled back, and someone—possibly Marya, possibly the young maid—had picked another rosebud and put it in a small silver vase on the table. Sara touched the silken petals with her forefinger, almost deluding herself she caught a faint, sweet, old-fashioned scent.

Tears clotted her throat. Nothing's changed, she told herself fiercely. And if the test had been positive you'd be shattered.

But she sat down on the side of the bed, letting herself mourn everything she'd lost.

Sheer, stubborn willpower brought it to an end. She swallowed, poured herself a glass of water from the jug on the bedside table, and forced herself to drink it down. Then, ferociously blinking back the moisture in her eyes, she inspected the room with careful detachment.

At least she could take some satisfaction with what she'd done there.

In spite of the too-white walls, it now looked authentic, she thought tiredly. Gone was the pretentious second-rate atmosphere, the cheap attempt at sophistication and luxury. Now nothing was superfluous; once the stone pine walls were returned to their original mellow gold, nothing would grate. The uncomplicated furniture and exquisite hangings and bedcover, the chandelier, newly polished by Marya and reinstalled by the castle handyman, fitted the ambience, as did the lamps on either side of the bed and the magnificent Persian carpet.

But other decorators would have done this as well as she

had—perhaps better. Others would now finish the redecoration. Gabe wouldn't want any reminders of her in the castle.

As soon as she got out of here she was going back to Fala'isi, the one place she could call home.

And if that made her defeated, well, so be it. She crawled into bed, pulled the covers over herself and let dull misery lull her into a kind of resignation.

CHAPTER ELEVEN

HER breakfast was delivered the following morning; dismayed, Sara sat up and glanced at her watch as the maid approached the bed.

'I didn't know it was so late!' she exclaimed.

The maid grinned and deposited the tray on her lap. 'OK,' she said cheerfully, then smiled again and nodded at the tray. 'For you.'

Sara looked down, flushing when she saw the note there, her name written in Gabe's strong handwriting.

She waited until she was alone before opening it. No salutation, no signature, just an impersonal, businesslike statement.

I'll come to your room in half an hour.

She leapt out of bed.

Half an hour later she'd forced down toast and coffee and an orange, showered and dressed in jeans and a jersey and her boots, and tied her hair back from her face in a very unsophisticated ponytail.

Although she'd also gone through a set of breathing exercises that were supposed to keep her calm, when she heard Gabe's knock on her door any benefit was lost in a rush of pure adrenalin.

'Come in,' she said, unclenching the hands at her sides and hoping he hadn't heard the betraying quiver in her voice.

Tall and dark and dominant, he walked into her room, his ice-blue eyes hooded and his mouth severe. 'Good morning,' he said formally.

His tone, his air, were like a slap in the face. 'Good morning,' she returned, adding with a stark intensity that hid her bitterness, 'The test was negative, you'll be pleased to know.'

Not a muscle moved in his handsome face, yet she sensed a hardening in him, a cold determination that sent a chill through her.

He didn't answer directly. 'Can you come down to my office, please?' he said. 'There are things we need to discuss.'

What on earth…? 'Your cousin—'

'Is talking to his wife on the telephone.'

An inexorable note in his voice warned her; she was going to have this discussion whether she wanted it or not. Anyway, she thought defiantly as she walked beside him down the stone-flagged passages, why should she shrink from this? Gabe couldn't hurt her any more than he already had.

But, oh, how she wished they hadn't made love; before, she'd been aware of him, but now with every breath she took she felt his presence as though he'd somehow invaded her body, marking her for all time as his possession. She could even taste him in her mouth….

Another person waited in the office, looking uneasy and stiff. And on the desk stood the leather coffer that held the priceless Queen's Blood, its lid open to reveal the brilliant cabochon-cut rubies in their chain of gold, each crimson dome glowing in the morning sunshine. Beautiful and barbaric, it possessed an aura that drew every eye.

Sara's gasp was audible. 'Oh, thank God,' she breathed, almost giddy with relief.

'Marya has something to tell you,' Gabe said evenly.

The elderly maid looked at him, and then at Sara, her expression so woebegone Sara felt an involuntary pang of sympathy.

'Tell her,' Gabe ordered.

She began to speak in hesitant Illyrian, but Gabe interrupted. 'In English,' he said, his voice so icily aloof that Sara flinched.

Marya looked sideways at Sara and muttered miserably, 'I took the Queen's Blood.'

'I know,' Sara said quietly, without looking at Gabe. 'Why?'

The old woman sighed. 'A test. The Queen set the Wolf three tests, to see if he…if he…' Searching for the right word, she glanced imploringly at Gabe and said something in Illyrian.

'Honourable,' he supplied, his tone giving nothing away. He looked at Sara. 'I told you the story of the Queen who died on the mountain and was transformed into a sprite?'

Sara nodded, wondering whether she'd by mischance stumbled into some Mediterranean fable.

'Honourable,' Marya said, nodding eagerly. 'After she marry him—still looking like old woman—like me!' She gestured at herself and gave a lopsided smile. 'The first test. But on wedding day he kiss young, beautiful woman—his…' She hesitated, then gave Gabe another beseeching look.

He said crisply, 'His cousin, apparently, but the Queen thought she was his mistress. That night, before they became true man and wife, she showed herself in all her beauty and then disappeared. Presumably in a puff of smoke, although no one has ever said so. However, she left the Queen's Blood behind, because she loved him.'

Sara frowned. 'You didn't tell me—'

His shoulders lifted in a shrug. 'I didn't think you'd be interested.'

When the silence grew too long she said, 'I'm not sure I understand. I thought the Queen—sprite, whatever—was an ancestor.'

'She was. The rest of the story details how the first Wolf fought for his love and eventually won her and happiness by passing the tests she set him. Marya felt that I should be tested,' Gabe said, adding indifferently, 'A test I clearly failed. All right, Marya, you can go. But first you have an apology to make.'

With dignity, Marya said, 'I am sorry to make you unhappy. But you are strong woman—and always best to know the truth.'

What on earth did she mean? Sara said, 'Why have you confessed now?'

Marya looked at Gabe, who translated. She shrugged. 'You leaving, so all over. Not good to go in anger. Not good for you, not good for him.'

'That's enough.' Gabe's voice was glacial.

Mind churning, Sara watched the maid leave the room, shrunken but indomitable.

She had so desperately wanted to know why Marya had stolen the necklace, but the explanation didn't answer any questions.

Gabe said with formidable restraint, 'I have to apologise, too.'

An apology would change nothing. Everything had been tainted by his distrust.

On the other hand, how would she have felt if she'd found Gabe in a similar situation?

Struggling to rise above the black void of her own emotions, she said huskily, 'Strangely enough, I'm glad she told you in the end. Why did she?'

'Because she knew I was sending you away for good today,' he said grimly.

She made a startled little sound, and he went on. 'I had no right to bring you here. My own strategy has rebounded on me, and it serves me right. I know it's too late, and this sounds like an excuse, but possibly if I'd grown up here I'd have had some understanding of why Marya felt our relationship should be tested. I'm sorry.'

Exhausted, she gave a listless shrug. 'I suppose she was right in the long run—it's better to know the truth.'

'I'm not entirely sure what she—or you—mean by that.'

The satirical edge to the words lit a flame of anger in the wasteland of her emotions. 'Well, when it came to the crunch you didn't trust me enough to believe me, did you?'

He said curtly, 'There was a reason.' But the statement sounded flat and unconvincing.

'So give it to me.'

Gabe looked at her, and in spite of the total mess he'd made of everything his body stirred. Even with smoky shadows beneath her glorious eyes, her beauty wielded too much power over him.

Without thinking, he said, 'It doesn't matter.'

Her brows shot up and she looked at him with such utter disbelief that he made an abrupt and probably stupid decision. He turned and opened a drawer, taking out the envelope he'd kept there for the past year—kept, but never opened again after the first time.

She gave him a startled glance when he handed it over, but took it, saying uncertainly, 'What is this?'

'Open it.'

With concentrated attention Gabe watched her face as she opened the flap and pulled out the glossy print, scanning her features for any change of expression, any sign of guilt or shame.

Instead, her brow wrinkled, and the only emotion he could see was complete astonishment, as though she couldn't believe what she saw there.

But when she looked up her eyes were blazing, and in a voice that shook with outrage she said, 'What the hell *is* this?'

'Notice the time and date,' he said, some dispassionate part of him admiring her acting ability.

She looked down. Silence, taut as a bowstring, stretched between them, sharp with unspoken emotions. The colour faded from her skin, leaving her white and suddenly haggard.

Her voice uneven and thin, she said, 'This—this travesty purports to be taken the night of your cousin's wedding—the night Marya took the Queen's Blood.'

'At two in the morning, to be exact,' he returned deliberately. 'Just after Marya "discovered" that the Queen's Blood had gone.' He paused, and when she didn't say anything he added in a voice so coldly sarcastic that she flinched, 'I may have been extraordinarily stupid, but it doesn't take much intuition to guess how you and Hawke planned to occupy the rest of the night.'

She'd been shaking her head as though she couldn't believe it, but at his words she looked up, her eyes huge in her pale face, her mouth trembling. 'So this is why you were so sure I'd stolen the necklace. Why didn't you tell me?'

He shrugged. 'Pride,' he told her laconically, adding

with lacerating self-derision, 'I have as little liking as any man for being made a cuckold.'

Sara swallowed. Her pictured face wavered in front of her eyes. The photograph was explicit; Hawke Kennedy was holding her in his arms, looking at her with an expression that could have been desire. She was looking at him with what certainly appeared to be incredulous eagerness. And they were both naked—except that those weren't her breasts, and she'd be prepared to bet that they weren't Hawke's shoulders, either. He'd been fully clothed, and she'd been wearing a wrap.

'It's a fake,' she said hoarsely, and let the photograph flutter to the ground as though it soiled her fingertips.

'Do you think I didn't have it checked?'

She shook her head again, stopping when she saw the hard constriction of his mouth. Why bother trying to make him see the truth when he so obviously didn't want to? Lassitude crept through her, clouding her mind. 'Where did you get it?'

'A paparazzo had staked out your bedroom, presumably stuck up a tree somewhere in the garden with a telephoto lens. I imagine he wanted photographs of us together.' His thin smile slashed at her. 'Instead, he got this—you and Hawke Kennedy, naked in each other's arms. I imagine he couldn't believe his luck, and, being astute, he surmised he could well get more from me than from the newspapers. He was right.'

At least, she thought with an odd lift of her heart, she now knew why he'd so flatly refused to believe her.

'You were cheated. But Marya was right; it's always better to know the truth.' She swallowed, calling on the last fragile remnants of pride to help her make it out of here. 'Our marriage wouldn't have stood a chance even if she hadn't got hung up on her old fairytales and the paparazzo hadn't doctored that photo. I wonder how many other people he's done private deals with.'

Although she kept her eyes fixed on some ancestor on the wall, she sensed Gabe's predatory stillness. Adrenalin returned in another rush.

'So nothing has changed? You deny this?'

She turned to stare him straight in the eye. 'I do deny it—absolutely and with as much conviction as I denied stealing the Queen's Blood,' she said steadily, her heart beginning to thump unevenly as he started towards her, the strong male contours of his face hardened by anger and contempt.

Instinctively her arms came up to ward him off. 'Don't you touch me!'

He stopped so close to her that she could smell him, the faint, disturbing scent almost overpowering her willpower. Emotions raged through her, but she couldn't let him take her in disdain again.

'Are you trying to tell me that you don't feel anything for me?' he asked, the sardonic gleam in his narrowed eyes making her feel gauche and foolish.

'Beyond lust?' she fired back, desperate to protect herself. 'Yes, you can kiss me into submission. That means nothing, and you know it—otherwise you wouldn't be sending me away.'

His magnetism surrounded her, splintering her defences as he bent the full force of his formidable will on her. But this time she would not surrender. Physical longing, addiction—whatever this was—might be powerful, but not as powerful as love.

And Gabe had never spoken of love.

He didn't speak of it now. Instead he turned away, as

though the sight of her was distasteful, and said, 'Tell me one thing—how long had you been sleeping with Kennedy?'

How glad she was that she hadn't given in!

'The only time I touched him was when he gave me a hug after telling me that the Queen's Blood was gone,' she said woodenly. 'Presumably that's what the photographer caught. I don't care whether you believe it or not.'

The silence in the room became oppressive. Sara stared blindly at the bank of computers, the high-tech paraphernalia of modern business, jarring and anachronistic against the massive stone walls and the vaulted arcade outside. Gabe might look like a twenty-first-century magnate who'd made his fortune using the most up-to-date information, but at heart he was like his forebears, a battle-hardened warrior with a fiercely territorial attitude.

'Your clothes are already being packed,' he said at last, his voice so cold she felt it to the marrow of her bones. 'The jet will take you to London.'

'Thank you,' she said, and turned and walked out of the room and out of his life.

He made no effort to keep her. Why should he? What he got from her was available from any number of women.

Back in the room she thought of now as hers, she found her suitcase open on the bed and someone too familiar packing her clothes.

'What are you doing here?' she asked Marya bluntly.

The maid cast her a look of entreaty, and to Sara's astonishment began to weep, her face wrinkling up as the tears slid down her cheeks.

Sharply, the words tumbling over each other, Sara demanded, 'What is it, Marya? What's the matter?'

'I am wrong,' Marya sobbed. 'I not know—' Her English degenerated into choked words that Sara couldn't make out.

'Sit down,' she said gently, pushing her onto the side of the bed and snatching up a box of tissues. 'Here, wipe your eyes and tell me what's happened. Has Gabe sacked you?'

Marya gulped and hiccuped and blew her nose. 'He not love you,' she wailed into the tissue. 'But you love him. His other women—not love him like you. So I want him to know—in his heart—' she struck her own chest with vigour '—how precious you are—to him. To test him,' she repeated, as though the words were a charm.

Sara nodded. Yet, although Marya had realised that something was wrong with their relationship, she didn't understand that Gabe's desire was based on nothing more than a raging carnality that would have burned out within months.

'Go on,' she said quietly, walking across to the armoire to pull out the skirt she'd worn that first night.

Settling down enough to twist the tissue in her work-hardened hands, Marya leaned forward and said earnestly, 'And he unhappy when you go—went,' she corrected herself. 'I thought, Soon he know she never steal the Queen's Blood. But no—so he don't love you? Better to know before than after the wedding. I wait and wait. Then going to tell him where the Queen's Blood is. But then he bring you here, so he love you.' She stared at Sara accusingly. 'But it all go wrong! Even after you share a bed it go wrong!'

Colour stung Sara's cheekbones. 'Because he doesn't love me.' She folded the skirt and put it in her case, each small, practised movement an echo of finality.

'He does, he does!' Marya insisted. 'I see him look at you—and none of his other women he look at like that.' She took a deep breath and calmed herself—and her syntax—down. 'But he is Considine—face like fallen angel and will of iron, and too many women wanting his money and his body and his power!' She darted a glance at Sara. 'He afraid.'

'Gabe?' Sara barely managed to rein in a hysterical bout of laughter. 'He doesn't know what the word means.'

Marya screwed up her face. 'You wrong, too. He knows. I tell him,' she said, scrambling to her feet. 'And then you will stay, and he will be happy, and the Queen happy, too.'

Sara whirled around. 'I know you love and respect him, but you don't know him, Marya. I'm not staying. And trying to convince him that he's in love with me will only make him angry. It wouldn't make any difference anyway, because I won't marry a man who doesn't trust me enough to believe me.'

Marya looked thoughtfully at her, then broke into a small, faintly smug smile. 'Yes,' she said simply. 'You are right. Of course.'

She went across to the armoire and took out the rest of the clothes. 'Now I pack your bag,' she said with a quick return of her autocratic air. 'The helicopter here soon.'

It was. Clad in black jeans and jacket, their sombreness relieved by a dusky rose T-shirt and a jaunty hat with a brim wide enough to hide her eyes, Sara slung her tote bag over her shoulder and went down to the courtyard with the man-servant and Marya.

The chopper descended with a whirr of noise and flying leaves. 'Thank you,' she said, smiling briefly at the old woman who'd done what she had for reasons she'd thought good enough.

Sara hadn't needed to wear the hat: Gabe didn't emerge to say goodbye. She climbed in, strapped the seat belt around her narrow waist and looked straight ahead as the helicopter took off.

In London, she handed over her plans for the three bedrooms in the Wolf's Lair, then resigned from her job.

'Pity,' her employer said, glancing up from her sketches. He gave her a brief, curious smile. 'I assume Considine told you of our arrangement?'

'Yes.' She kept her voice level, but enough of her distaste and outrage showed in her tone to make him blink.

'I thought you'd be a total loss,' he said mildly. 'But you've got talent. Your position's still open if you want it—and this time Considine won't have anything to do with it.'

'No, thanks.'

'Then I'll write you a good reference.'

Sara almost told him what he could do with his reference, but common sense stayed her tongue. She needed it; she'd have no chance of getting a decent job without one. 'Thank you,' she said tonelessly.

'Where do you plan to go?'

'America,' she said quickly, without thinking.

'New York? L.A.?'

She shrugged. 'Los Angeles—the weather's better.'

'I'm sorry,' he said unexpectedly.

She was, too, but she smiled and shook her head. 'Don't be—it's been excellent experience,' she said ironically.

CHAPTER TWELVE

GETTING to Fala'isi used up every cent in Sara's bank account and pushed her credit card to the limit, and the journey turned into an endurance test. But she finally made it, sinking exhausted and gritty-eyed into a taxi just after midnight, island time.

'Have a good trip?' the driver enquired. A man she didn't recognise, he'd been waiting at the airport, brandishing a sign with her name written on it. She'd winced, because she'd hoped to slink in without notice, and on Fala'isi news travelled at the speed of light.

Not that Gabe would ever know or care where she'd gone.

'A long one,' she told the driver, wishing the cab had air-conditioning.

'Oh? You get caught up in the strike in New Zealand?'

'Yes.'

And before that there'd been a delay and eventual cancellation in Los Angeles. From there she'd had to island-hop to Hawaii, and then across the equator to Tahiti and Rarotonga—magical islands lying in a sunlit sea—before heading south to New Zealand to pick up the jet for Fala'isi.

Weariness sucked her down into a grey misery, weighting down her bones and clogging her brain. Normally she'd have loved the roundabout journey; at the moment all she wanted to do was go to bed and sleep for three weeks.

Or three years, she thought satirically. But she suspected that even then she'd wake up still loving Gabe.

The driver asked, 'You been here before?'

'Yes.' Shortly after her twenty-first birthday she'd used the legacy from her grandparents to come back and renew acquaintance with an old school friend who rented out two small cottages right on the lagoon.

Nonchalantly swerving to avoid a small motor scooter with three people on board, the driver enquired, 'Stayed at the same place then?'

'Yes,' she admitted.

'Nice little house, that, right on the beach. My cousin owns it—she told me to pick you up.'

And Tarifa would have aired the cottage and made the bed and filled the fridge with food. 'It was good to see you,' Sara said woodenly. 'Sorry, I'm not thinking too well at the moment.'

He laughed, a rich, full sound that embodied the Pacific. 'You need a holiday! And you've come to the right place for it.'

Once inside the house, she felt painful tears sting her eyes when she saw that the hibiscus flowers so carefully arranged on the table were dead, their vibrant silken petals faded into crumpled tissue.

A week ago she'd been in the Wolf's Lair, futilely hoping that she could make Gabe realise that she would never have stolen from him.

Hoping, she realised now, that he felt more for her than passion.

Well, he didn't, and although in his arms she became a different, rapturously transformed being, it wasn't enough.

Without love and trust and friendship, passion was just a cruel fantasy, a craving that promised everything only to leave her unfulfilled and heartsick.

The humid air pressed onto her, thick and hot, perfumed with the sweetness of frangipani, its elusive, erotic scent mingling with the fresh, salty tang of the sea.

She pushed the shutters back and opened the doors out onto the terrace that overlooked the beach. Far out on the lagoon, lights flickered—fishermen catching food for their families.

From behind her, Gabe said, 'You took long enough to get here.'

Gasping, she spun on her heel, incredulous eyes stretching wide at the sight of him standing in the doorway. Panic kicked viciously in her stomach.

'What—?' She closed her eyes, but his dominant figure was still burned into her retinas. Hoarsely, she forced herself to demand, 'What are you doing here?'

'Your landlady gave me a key.'

'She had no right.'

Yet she couldn't blame Tarifa—Gabe in full charm mode was irresistible, and the hint of steel behind the compelling magnetism would have won Tarifa over in a second. Gathering what was left of her composure, Sara ploughed on, 'I thought I'd made it plain that I won't be your mistress, or your lover, or whatever you want me to be.'

'I want you to be my wife,' he said harshly.

She stared at him, feeling the world wobble under her feet. He didn't look like a man who'd just proposed; in a face more austere than she'd ever seen it, his eyes were hooded against her, and a muscle flickered on the autocratic line of his jaw.

Although temptation dangled like a glittering bauble in

front of her, she summoned just enough despairing courage to reject it. 'Get out,' she whispered, and then, more strongly, 'Get out of here!'

He said roughly, 'At least let me say I'm sorry.'

'I'll take it as said.' Already she could feel herself weakening, feel her love making false promises, trying to convince her that it didn't matter that he hadn't trusted her. 'Now, go!'

The room wavered in front of her eyes, coalescing into a hideously nauseating whirl. The last thing she heard was Gabe swearing in Illyrian as she let herself tip over into the refuge of unconsciousness.

She woke wondering where she was, before memory forced its way back. Her eyes flew open and she bolted up off the bed. Her head spun and she was clutching the head-rail when Gabe came in through the door, a glass of water in his hand.

'Lie down!' he ordered, his strides lengthening. He caught her in one strong hand, then set the glass on the bedside table.

She stood limply, shaking her head as the walls began to sway again.

'Lie down, Sara!'

But she didn't dare move. Gabe said something else under his breath and picked her up.

With her cheek pressed against his chest, and the rapid beat of his heart echoing in her ears, she thought dreamily that it was like coming home again after years in exile.

Closing her eyes in mute surrender, she accepted then that she couldn't resist him. Whatever he wanted from her she would give, because she loved him so intensely it physically hurt.

'How long is it since you've had anything to eat or drink?' Gabe's voice resonated through her head as he pulled the sheet back.

'I don't know.' The words sounded thick and slurred. 'I've been drinking water.'

'I don't blame you for not wanting to eat airline food,' he said grimly, lowering her back onto the bed, 'but starving yourself for three days is plain stupid. I notice someone's left a bowl of fruit for you in the kitchen. I'll get you a banana—that should help your blood sugar.'

The thought of forcing anything down her constricted throat brought another spasm of nausea, but he was right; she was running on empty, and if she didn't get something into her stomach she'd faint again. She shut her eyes and tried to breathe slowly and deeply.

Although she kept her lashes clamped down when the mattress depressed under Gabe's weight, every sense sprang to painful alertness, banishing the lassitude of a moment ago.

'Bite,' he ordered.

Obediently she bit into the sweet, soft flesh of the little lady's finger banana.

'Now, chew. And then swallow.'

Sara did as she was told before croaking indignantly, 'I know how to eat.'

'Then why haven't you been doing it?' he asked unanswerably. 'It's seventy-two hours since you left London, and I'll bet you haven't had anything to eat in that time.'

She'd have answered, but the banana was once again pressed against her lips. And, because it was piercingly sweet to be cared for by him, she forced the fruit past the obstruction in her throat.

He got up. 'I'll make a cup of tea and you can drink that, and then you can have a shower. However much water you've drunk, you probably need rehydrating from the skin in.'

The banana provided enough energy for her to manoeuvre herself up against the pillows; she was glowering at the door when he came back in carrying a large mug.

He glanced at the water he'd brought in before, and nodded. 'Good, you've drunk it. Now, get this down.'

'I won't be told what to do in my own house,' she said, but her voice was tired and lacklustre.

'Not only will I tell you, if necessary I'll make you,' he said mildly, and held out the mug. 'Is this too heavy for you?'

'No.'

The tea was milky and overly sweet, but she drank it down greedily.

'That's better,' he said when she'd finished. 'You've got a bit of colour back in your cheeks.'

Only, she thought wearily, because he was sitting beside her and her racing heart was pumping blood through her body. Exhausted and jet-lagged, she still responded to his overwhelming male charisma.

'It's not fair,' she said woodenly. 'I can't fight you, but I don't want you here.'

'Don't worry, you'll be ready for another bout in the morning. You just need twelve hours' sleep and some decent food,' he said with an odd, cynical smile. 'As for getting rid of me—not tonight. You're still shaky and you need looking after. Do you think you can walk to the bathroom?'

'I don't want to.' The energy provided by the banana and the sugar in the tea was proving very temporary. Oblivion beckoned like some dark, voracious tunnel, promising her a few precious hours when she wouldn't have to deal with anything.

Gabe's will defeated her. 'You'll feel better if you have a shower.'

The next moment she was being lifted into the air. She

opened her eyes to meet his, steel-blue and utterly determined.

'Relax,' he said on an amused note, and carried her into the tiny bathroom.

Limply she endured it, but when he sat her down on a chair and started on the buttons of her shirt she said, 'No!' and her hand came up to hold his still, her eyes enormous in her white face.

'I'm not going to do anything beyond showering you,' he said, in a voice that shattered the fragile remnants of her composure.

'I can do it myself,' she said stubbornly, clinging to what little pride she had left.

He paused, then stood up. 'All right.'

But he didn't go, and one glance at his uncompromising expression convinced her that any further objection on her part was useless. Grimly ignoring him, she undid the rest of her shirt. The tie on her loose cotton trousers proved more difficult, but she wrestled it undone and stood up, letting the trousers drop to her feet. Yet another wave of faintness took her by surprise; head swimming, she clutched the back of the chair and tried to breathe evenly.

Unceremoniously Gabe picked her up and dumped her into the shower.

The water on Fala'isi was never cold, but the lukewarm spray hit her like bullets. She gasped, and while she was adjusting to the blissful wetness he stripped her bra and pants away and got in himself, still fully clothed, and began washing her.

She shuddered at the smooth, skillful caress of his hands as he soaped and rinsed. What little strength she had left seeped away with the grime of her long flight, so that by the time he reached over and turned off the water she was lying back against the hard support of his body, so relaxed she couldn't have moved if she'd tried.

Her brain had gone to sleep. Afterwards she could dimly remember him drying her, but the journey back into the bedroom was a blank, and as jet-lagged sleep claimed her she didn't know that tears were seeping through her lashes.

She woke to warmth, to darkness, and the slow, steady beat of a heart, the exquisite pleasure of being held against a lean, strongly muscled body—woke to that inevitable sense of rightness, of completion, that told her she was with Gabe, and that she'd spent the night locked in his arms.

For long seconds she lay there, still under the influence of the cloudy shadows that had been her dreams. Without moving, keeping her breathing steady, she opened her eyes. The moon had set, and it was dark and still and silent, the only sound the ever-present rumble of the waves on the outer reef.

And the deep, regular sound and movement of Gabe's breath. His eyes were closed, his body lax in the abandon of sleep, but the arm around her held her close, as though she were infinitely precious. Her mouth trembled into a wistful smile.

Why had he come?

Sara didn't dare to hope. She banished the question from her mind and let herself dwell only on the present moment, that infinitely small space of time she had with the man she loved.

Her muscles demanded a good stretch, but that would wake Gabe.

The soft whisper of air from the fan above the bed brushed across her sensitised skin, mingling with the salty breath of the sea. Shutting her eyes again, she abandoned herself to imprinting every tiny sensory detail on her mind so firmly that she'd never forget. When she was an old woman she wanted to be able to recall everything—the scent of him, the slow, even rise and fall of his chest against her, the texture of his hot, sleek skin against her naked body, the exact distance from his waist to his hip....

Hardly breathing, she inched her hand over the centre of his chest, feeling his formidable life force drive into her palm. He didn't move. Bolder now, but still cautious, she eased her head around to kiss his shoulder. When he didn't respond she let her lips linger, her tongue taste him, her senses bask in lazy, sleepy appreciation of the man she loved.

Normally, she thought dreamily, he woke at the slightest touch. She couldn't be the only one with jet-lag. She lowered her hand to his waist, and felt the band of something that felt like shorts.

It was perilously sweet to lie here with him at her mercy, but it seemed cheating, somehow. He'd been kind to her, he'd fed her and bathed her, and kept the darkness at bay with the comfort of his body, but that didn't give her the right to touch him while he slept.

Yet her hand strayed back to cover his heart, and she kept her face turned into his shoulder, hardly breathing in case he woke, drifting in a nebulous never-never land where dreams might come true.

Just a few moments more, she thought drowsily...and slid back to sleep, to the most erotic dream she'd ever had.

'Awake?' Gabe's voice was barely audible, but it brought her to full alertness.

The bed beneath her moved; her eyes flew open as Gabe's arms tightened around her. She was, she realised, stretched out along him with her face tucked into his neck.

His powerful thighs shifted beneath her, revealing that he was very, very aroused.

Oh, what had she done?

In her dream she'd made slow, patient love to him, using every skill he'd taught her, every subtle sexual nuance to arouse him. Only it seemed that her dream had become reality, because her own body was singing with delighted anticipation, every cell alight with desire.

Hot with embarrassment, she muttered, 'Yes,' and tried to slither off him.

His arms tightened. In a raspy, after-sleep voice he asked, 'Know where you are?'

'Fala'isi.'

'Know who you're with?'

Her head came up fast, connecting with his chin. 'Of course I do.'

'Say my name.'

She opened reluctant eyes to broad daylight, blinking at the bright sun-stripes across the floor through the shutters. A fierce joy burned through her; Gabe's angular features were drawn in the stark lines of desire.

'Why?' she demanded.

'Because I want to be sure that you know what you're doing.' His face hardened. 'I didn't realise you were asleep when you woke me with such charming caresses, so if you want to stop now that you're awake, this is your last chance.'

Sara didn't hesitate. 'I don't want to stop.' She lowered her lips, and a hair's breadth away from his she said, 'You're Gabe.'

My only love....

Harshly he said, 'Then take me, Sara.'

Sara froze, and time stretched into silence until she straightened up to look down into his beloved face. She wanted to make sure that he'd never forget this, that every time he lay like this with any other woman it would be her face he saw with those narrowed, glittering eyes, her name that echoed through his mind, her taste in his mouth.

His brows drew together. 'Are you all right?'

'Never better,' she vowed huskily, and began to play the seductress in earnest, using her body to set the pace, to stake a subtle claim.

A claim he'd probably choose not to recognise.

It didn't matter. He was her other half, the only man who complemented her and made her whole. Oh, she could live without him—she'd have to—but it would be a life without savour and love.

She half expected him to resist when he realised what she was doing, but he didn't; although she saw the immense effort it took him to lock his muscles and lie still, he gave her the freedom of his body.

Letting her emotions tell her what to do, how to do it, she leashed the heady clamour of desire that urged her to take swift satisfaction, and pleasured them both into a dreamy sensuous madness as the tropical day burned into afternoon.

Until Gabe said in a constricted, goaded voice, 'Any more of this torment, you witch, and I won't last!'

Yet still he didn't reach for her, didn't seize control. By then the time for sensuous deliberation was past for her, too; she wanted nothing more than the consummation that beckoned so urgently.

She took him into her, moving with fierce energy as her tight inner muscles clasped and clung, and almost instantly she soared to a rapture so intense she almost blacked out when at last she surrendered to it.

Hands clamped on her thighs, his eyes blazing blue, Gabe followed her there. A low, harsh sound surged up from deep in his throat and his magnificent body arced beneath her like a bow.

Sara collapsed bonelessly onto him, listening to the thunder of his heart as his arms clamped around her. When his breathing had steadied enough for him to be able to speak, he said, 'Food. You need food.'

His protectiveness touched her, but… *I need you*, she thought, listening to her own heartbeat as a drifting melancholy stole over her.

He lifted her chin, searching her face with hooded eyes. '*Need* me?' he said harshly.

Humiliation swept across her. Oh, God, she'd actually said it. She closed her eyes against his unsparing gaze and burrowed into his chest, her mind racing frantically for some way of undoing the damage.

And then she lifted her head and confronted him. 'Yes,' she said simply.

He reversed their positions in one swift, powerful movement. 'Like this?' he asked between his teeth, and took her with a single, desperate thrust.

She welcomed him with joy—with joy and rapture and relief. Exquisite sensations flooded through her and her tight inner muscles clamped around him.

If this was all he had to offer, she'd take it. 'Yes,' she breathed, looping her arms around his neck to hold him close.

But from then on he moved with tormenting gentleness, as though she was infinitely precious and fragile, forcing her to accept a much slower, somehow more intimate conquest than the swift, fierce conflagration she'd anticipated.

Paying her back, she thought. But this was such sweet revenge….

Panting, her heart thundering in her ears and the blood

coursing through her body, she discovered again the addictive pleasures of being held in his arms while he worked his sensual magic.

Yet her second climax took her by surprise, shattering her with its consuming elemental power. Her body twisted into the hard length of his and her hands fell away from his shoulders, clenching and unclenching on the sheets as waves of erotic pleasure spread from her core, drowning out everything but the sharp ecstasy of release.

She called out his name, his arms tightened around her and he spilled into her, and together they clung until the ecstasy faded into a sense of profound fulfilment.

Eventually Gabe moved, ignoring her muted protest to turn onto his side and scoop her to lie on top of him. She stretched languorously and listened to his heartbeat, solid, steady, and infinitely comforting.

'Go back to sleep,' he commanded, his tone rough.

And she did, losing herself in bittersweet dreams until she woke again. This time she was alone in the bed, and her panicked reaction told her more than she wanted to accept about her complete capitulation.

Unwillingly she forced her eyelids up. The room was empty, and the bright, flamboyant sky through the shutters told her that sunset was approaching.

Had Gabe gone? She turned over onto her stomach, burying her face in the pillow while questions hammered at her brain. What was he doing here? Had he really asked her to be his wife?

No, that must have been a hallucination. But making love hadn't been. She stretched, relishing the pull of rarely used muscles, the sleek, languorous satisfaction in every cell.

So—what was going to happen now? Why had he come all the way across the world? She'd have bet her life that he'd had no intention of doing that when she'd left the Wolf's Lair.

A few seconds later she sensed that he'd returned; carefully she turned her head and sneaked a glance from between her lashes, her heart bolting when she saw him put a jug of water onto the bedside table. His tall presence was a shadow, and the rapidly approaching dusk hid the expression on his face, but she sensed that he'd retreated into himself, shutting her out.

Pouring out a glass, he said quietly, 'How do you feel?'

Terrified—yet fighting back a wild, persistent hope. But that wasn't what he wanted to know. 'Much better, thank you.'

She accepted the glass gratefully and let the cold iced water trickle down her throat with sensuous appreciation.

'You sound like a small girl after a party.' He paused, then said in a completely different tone, 'I can't ask for forgiveness, but I'm sorry I didn't trust you enough to believe that you hadn't stolen the Queen's Blood.'

Sara swallowed down the last of the water and stood the glass on the table. 'It's all right,' she said. 'I understand why. The last thing you'd have expected was for Marya to decide to set you a test!'

His mouth tightened. 'I hope I'd have believed you if it hadn't been for that damned photograph.'

Sara looked up into his face, the bone structure more dominant than usual, all hard angles and planes. Her passionate wildfire hope faded into ashes, cold and dark and useless. The photograph was always going to be between them, she knew—fake, but utterly damning.

He went on, 'It cut my pride to the quick and it reinforced your supposed guilt. Yet it was a complete coincidence. I'm almost beginning to believe Marya has it right—that the Queen is still watching over her valley and her descendants, setting tests like some ancient autocratic schoolmistress. It was certainly a test for me—another one I failed.'

Sara started to protest, but when he turned away she bit back the words, too afraid to hope, too afraid not to, knowing only that her future depended on the next few minutes.

Gabe stopped to stare through the window. The sun was ready to sink into oblivion below the horizon, but its dying brilliance flooded the world, light pouring through the wooden shutters to tiger-stripe his big lithe body in gold and dark bronze, to lovingly outline the powerful pull of muscle and sinew.

He said evenly, 'When I watched you march out of the castle, with your back straight and your shoulders set, I vowed that I'd never willingly set eyes on you again.' He swung around, fixing a fiercely intent gaze onto her face. 'But I kept thinking of the way you'd shielded that child in the village with your body, and your compassion for Marya in spite of what she'd done. And, although the photograph had been judged genuine by the expert I took it to, you'd shown no signs of being attracted to Hawke. Or he to you.'

She waited, heartbeats suspended, while from somewhere outside a *tikau* bird called, the mystical carillon of notes falling like silver bells on her ear. Rare, secretive, found only on Fala'isi, the bird was supposed to sing only to true lovers….

Gabe said abruptly, 'When you saw it, you looked shocked. Not guilty, not ashamed, not even self-conscious—just stunned and totally disbelieving. I told myself it was because you hadn't realised the paparazzo was there—but I had to admit that it could have been because it never happened.'

She wanted to tell him that the only time Hawke had

touched her was his brief, sympathetic hug, but some hidden instinct kept her silent.

In the same deep, deliberate voice, he went on, 'I reminded myself how wrong I'd been about the Queen's Blood. So I got in touch with the expert again. Then I came here.'

'What did he—your expert—say?' Hardly daring to breathe, she waited for his answer.

'I haven't heard from him.' He shrugged. 'Apparently he's viewing it with an armoury of new tricks.'

Startled, she said, 'When will he know?'

'It doesn't matter.'

Had he gone mad? She repeated starkly, 'It doesn't *matter*?'

'Not any longer.' He paused. 'On the way here, I did something I should have done a year ago—I ignored my wounded pride and tried to think logically. In the end it came down to two things—your character, and the photograph. You prickle with independence—you wouldn't let me buy you clothes or shower you with gifts the way I wanted to. Even when we were lovers you wouldn't move in with me, and you kept working. All of which could have been because you were planning to steal the Queen's Blood, but you were transparently honest in your emotions, your reactions. I let myself believe that you were a thief because I didn't want to be in love with you.'

'I understand. I do,' she insisted when she saw disbelief twist his mouth. 'I didn't want to love you, either. It was—' she gestured widely '—too *big*. Too overwhelming—frightening. As for the photograph—well, I know how I'd feel if the situation were reversed, if I'd been shown a photograph of you holding another woman, both of you apparently naked. And Hawke is very dishy.'

His eyes narrowed, and she gave a wry smile. 'Come

on, Gabe—you know perfectly well that he's good-looking. But he's—' She stopped.

His eyes hardened. 'He's what?'

She said, 'I rather think your sister finds him very attractive.'

'Melissa?' His brows drew together. 'She's too young.'

'Gabe, she's twenty-two, plenty old enough to fall in love. And then there was the Queen's Blood—you see, because I hadn't taken it I knew it had to be Marya.'

'If that photograph hadn't arrived in my e-mail the day after the necklace had been stolen I mightn't have been so intransigent.'

'Why didn't you show me then?'

She held her breath until he said in a flat, aloof voice, 'I didn't want to see you again. Actually, I didn't dare see you again—I was afraid I might end up forgiving you. That's why I didn't tell you face-to-face that our engagement was over; I'd always rather prided myself on my strength of character, but I discovered the day after the theft that where you're concerned I have none. I'm sorry you had to learn it from my letter.'

She'd learned it from a press statement, waved in the hands of a journalist, but she wasn't going to tell him that now. Hardly daring to breathe, she waited for him to go on, his every word fanning the hope she'd thought so dead.

'Marya is completely convinced that the welfare of everyone in the valley and the castle depends on the happiness of each lord. So it's vital that his marriage is happy. And to be happy it has to be built on strong foundations.'

Mouth and throat dry, Sara waited for his next words. He spoke slowly, as though clarifying his inner thoughts. 'A year of hell,' he finished in a harsh undertone, 'because of a myth!'

'But it's not a myth for her, and probably not for most of the peasants,' Sara said quietly, skating over the surface of his words because she was too afraid to probe deeper. 'Listening to her tell the legend is like slipping back into the past, into a world where the sprite Queen guards her jewels for hundreds of years until her true love comes to claim her and them.'

He said tersely, 'If I'd known—if I'd been brought up in the Wolf's Lair like my father—perhaps I'd have understood how much of a hold the old story had on the people in the valley. But I didn't.'

Sara was silent, biting her lip to keep the words back. Marya had other reasons for her actions. She'd understood that although Sara loved Gabe, he didn't love her.

He caught her chin and tilted her face to meet his merciless gaze. 'What's going on behind that serene face?' he demanded.

'It's just that I understand. From Marya's point of view, she had everything covered. If you passed her test—if you trusted me enough to believe me—then we'd be happy together, which would mean security for the valley. If you didn't trust me, then you didn't love me, and the sooner we broke up the better for everyone. I can see her point.'

Eyes blazing with blue fire in his dark, astonished face, he let her go. 'Not love you?' He exploded. 'What the hell gave her that idea? Why would I have asked you to marry me if I hadn't loved you? She must be mad.'

As though he couldn't contain his energy, he strode across to the window and stood staring out across the lagoon.

Sara smiled sadly. 'She's a very astute woman. And she was right—if you'd loved me, you'd have believed me.'

The last edge of the sun moved below the horizon and dusk fell, abrupt and clinging, warm and seductive.

'She made it impossible!' Gabe ground out. 'I was certain Marya of all people wouldn't have stolen the necklace. And when I saw that photograph—I wanted to kill Kennedy. I couldn't think straight—I'd never felt such a fury of anger before. Damn it, no *reasonable* man would have believed that you were innocent!'

'But a man who loved me would have listened,' she pointed out quietly, her heart breaking again.

Tense silence echoed around the room. Again, Sara heard the exquisite trill of the secretive *tikau*. An ancient tradition on the island held that when two people heard it together they were fated to happiness.

Like so many ancient traditions, it didn't hold up in the light of day, she thought sadly.

At last Gabe said in a cool, judicial tone, 'Love isn't necessarily a lasting thing in my world. My parents weren't particularly happy; they stayed together for our sakes. It sounds conceited, but I've been a target since I grew up; the title was a magnet to some women, and the fact that I made a lot of money fast made me more of a prize. There was nothing personal in it.'

Sara said incredulously, 'If you really believe that, I have a bridge somewhere I can sell you!'

'I could be a metre tall and ugly and it would have made no difference,' he said cynically. 'Money is a great aphrodisiac. I've seen marriages splinter and crumble all around me all my life. I thought I wanted the moon—a love that was rock-solid and honest, based on something much stronger than passion. But then I met you and all my logical decisions flew out the nearest window. I had to have you.'

He gave a brief, tight smile. 'I lose control when I look at you. I wanted you beyond bearing, yet I felt that my complete absorption in you made me less of a man, as though I had no life apart from you. So I used the disappearance of the Queen's Blood as an excuse to regain my autonomy, and I seized on the photograph as reinforcement.'

She started to laugh and he swung around, his face set in lines of total hauteur.

Her laughter cracked, died away. 'I felt exactly the same,' she said, lips trembling. 'I thought that what we had was nothing more than sublime sex, and that when it faded—because that flashpoint of physical attraction does, doesn't it?—there'd be nothing but ashes.' But she'd loved him so much she'd been ready to risk it.

Finally Gabe said into the richly perfumed dusk, 'I was afraid.'

She tried to resist the cautious embers of hope that were warming her. 'Of what?'

'Of losing myself in you.' He shot her a smouldering glance over his shoulder before addressing the garden and the lagoon again. 'I'd never felt like that about anyone before. It's no excuse, and saying it sounds stupid, because now I know what life without you is like—sheer bloody desolation—but I didn't know how to handle it.'

Sara felt as though she'd been hit repeatedly about the head. 'You were angry.'

He sent her a startled look, then nodded. 'I'm used to being in control. My father died when I was nineteen, and I took over the family business and looking after Melissa and Marco. I had my life in perfect order. Then you walked into that party and stole my heart, and I couldn't do anything about it. I loved you from the moment I saw you, and every moment I spent with you just tipped me deeper and deeper into what I feared was obsession.'

He came back to the bed, grabbed the glass and poured

himself a drink. Sara shivered, torn between burgeoning hope and fear.

He said sombrely, 'Nevertheless, I had to ask you to marry me. When you said yes, I felt as though I'd conquered the world, but even then I must have been looking for a way out. So when Marya came up with her damned crackpot test, I thought that I'd mistaken lust for love. I was a coward.'

Sara closed her eyes, her stomach churning. Yes, she understood that; it had happened the same way for her, a swift immersion in the sea of love, and then that desperation, as though she was drowning in emotions too big, too unmanageable to cope with.

Outside, a gull screamed, harsh and defiant and aggressive. Into the silent air Gabe said quietly, 'And if the photograph hadn't sent me into a mindless jealous rage, I'd have been more reasonable.'

'So what are you going to do about it?'

'Don't worry,' he said with a coolly menacing smile. 'The photographer didn't get away with it.'

'I still can't believe that you paid him off.'

He hesitated, then said quietly, 'Sheer arrogant pride, I'm afraid. I hated the thought of the world looking at it.'

He switched on the lamp at the head of the bed. Sara shrank back into the tumbled pillows, feeling naked and exposed now that the friendly dusk had been banished.

Eyes searching and narrowed in his lean face, Gabe said, 'Last night I asked you to be my wife. It was the wrong time, and I'm sorry. But I'm asking again. Sara, marry me.'

She was stunned into silence. 'Why?' she finally managed to whisper. 'You don't have to—m-make things up to me—'

Frowning, he cut her off. 'I want you to marry me for a purely selfish reason—because I can't live without you. I love you, and I need you, and I trust you; I'll cherish you until I die.'

She smiled mistily at him, and sniffed as tears clogged her throat. Even when asking, he sounded autocratic and uncompromising, but she wouldn't have him any other way.

'Yes,' she said simply. 'Of course I'll marry you. Whenever and wherever you want me to. I love you.'

He bent and kissed her, a light, even tentative touch on her lips, so keenly sweet that she shivered beneath it.

'Not tears,' he muttered in a thick, impeded voice. 'Don't cry, my darling, my dear heart, my treasure. I can't give you back this last year, but I swear that from now on I'll make sure you never have cause to cry—'

He groaned and sank down beside her, and kissed her again, and this time it wasn't light or tentative at all.

Much later, he said into her hair, 'I wasn't going to make love to you. I spent last night planning to woo you without falling into bed with you, and look what happened. You're a dangerous woman, smashing all my good intentions with one sleepy kiss.'

She laughed and ran a fingertip the length of his chest, revelling in his suddenly shortened breath. 'I thought I was dreaming,' she confessed. 'When I woke up and—well, you know what I'd done—I felt so embarrassed I could have died. This will last, won't it?' she said, suddenly needing reassurance that things had changed, that, no matter how wonderful the sex, it was based on something stronger and more lasting.

His hand covered hers. 'Yes,' he said simply. 'This is heart-shakingly erotic, but we have much more than passion on which to build our life together. Where would you like to be married?'

'Why?' she asked.

He shrugged and kissed her forehead. 'Alex wants it to be in Illyria—a big, formal wedding with all the bells and whistles. But yesterday when I got here I discovered that we can marry within three days. Would you like to do that?'

She'd have loved to do that, but she said, 'Won't the people in the valley be disappointed?'

When he hesitated, she kissed him and said, 'We'll do the wedding in Illyria.'

'We can do both,' he said. 'This is your island, your home. If we have a private wedding here for us, then I can cope with waiting for the six months or so that it's going to take to organise the other.'

He reached out a long arm and groped in the drawer of the bedside table, withdrawing his hand to reveal something that glowed in the light of the lamp.

Sara's breath locked in her throat.

'Your ring,' he said in a deep voice.

Smiling mistily, she held out her hand. He slid the ruby onto her finger and kissed it, and then her.

'This time it comes with love and trust,' he said, making a vow of the simple words. 'Now, you must want something to eat.'

She kissed him and said, 'In a few minutes.'

And let her cheek drop to his chest, and lay listening to the mingled sound of their heartbeats. Dreamily, so happy it was difficult to formulate the words, she thought that every morning from now on she'd lie like this with Gabe, and know that they were safe with each other.

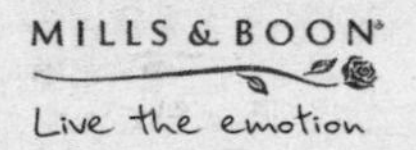

Modern romance™

BEDDED FOR REVENGE *by Sharon Kendrick*

Cesare's pride had been wounded but he planned to bed Sorcha, and then dump her…all for revenge! And revenge was sweet. Sorcha Whittaker was still the sexiest woman he'd ever seen, and their passion was incredible. The hard part now was walking away…

THE SECRET BABY BARGAIN *by Melanie Milburne*

Jake Marriott was clear about the terms of his relationships – no marriage, no babies. So Ashleigh Forrester ran because she was pregnant with his child. But Jake is back, and the striking resemblance to her son is too obvious to ignore. Now Jake wants to buy her as his wife…

MISTRESS FOR A WEEKEND *by Susan Napier*

Nora Lang wants the most dangerous man she can find! Enter top tycoon Blake Macleod. When Nora acquires some business information that he can't risk being leaked, Blake has to keep her in sight – he'll make love to her for the whole weekend!

TAKEN BY THE TYCOON *by Kathryn Ross*

Nicole and her handsome boss Luke Santana work hard and play hard, with no strings attached. But Nicole finds herself wanting more than Luke can give, so she ends their liaison. What will Luke do when he uncovers the secret Nicole carries with her now…?

On sale 4th August 2006

Available at WHSmith, Tesco, ASDA, Borders, Eason, Sainsbury's and most bookshops

www.millsandboon.co.uk

0606/108/MB038

Escape to...

19th May 2006

16th June 2006

21st July 2006

18th August 2006

Available at WH Smith, Tesco, ASDA, Borders, Eason, Sainsbury's and all good paperback bookshops

www.millsandboon.co.uk

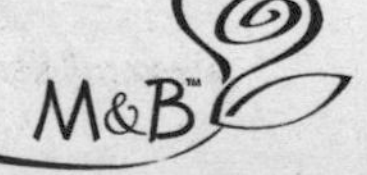